Del Río Hondo

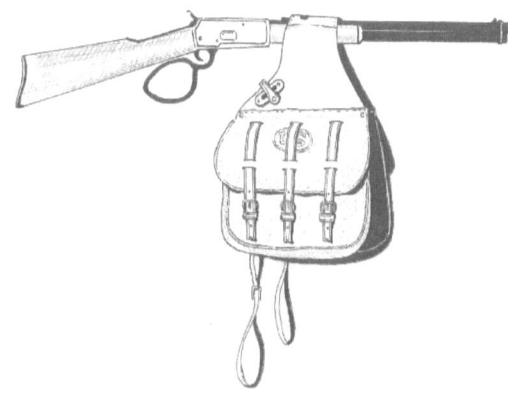

Vol. IV
West to Bravo series

Look for other Western & Adventure novels by
Eric H. Heisner

Along to Presidio

West to Bravo (I)

Seven Fingers a' Brazos (II)

Above the Llano (III)

T. H. Elkman

Mexico Sky

Short Western Tales: Friend of the Devil

Wings of the Pirate

Africa Tusk

Fire Angels

Cicada

Citation for Murder

Conch Republic, Island Stepping with Hemingway

Conch Republic – vol. 2, Errol Flynn's Treasure

Conch Republic – vol. 3, Coba Libre

Follow book releases and film productions at:
www.leandogproductions.com

Del Río Hondo

Eric H. Heisner

Illustrations by Al P. Bringas

Visit our website at
www.leandogproductions.com

Illustrations by: Al P. Bringas
Contact: al_bringas@yahoo.com

Dustcover jacket design: Dreamscape Cover Designs

Author photo by: Dan Farnam

Edited by: Story Perfect Editing Services – Tim Haughian

Paperback ISBN: 978-1-956417-30-2

Dedication

~ Texas ~
I have found me a home.

Special Thanks

Amber Word Heisner, Al P. Bringas,
Dan Farnam & Tim Haughian

Note from Author

Western stories have been a passion for me since I was a kid growing up in Illinois. My youth was spent running around a recreated Old West town while my college professor dad had a secret identity as a summer-stock gunfighter. Over the years, I started performing in shows and doing stunts, which led me to making Westerns in film school.

After living in Hollywood for a while, I eventually settled with my young family in Texas. Now, I go to my ranch in the Hill Country where my imagination runs wild, and the stories come to life. With this 4th story in the *West to Bravo* series, I'm glad to have you along, joining Holton, Jules, and Dog, for another journey through the western frontier.

As they say in show business – "Maybe it's not the way it was, but it's the way it should have been."

Eric H. Heisner

May 20, 2024

Chapter 1

A man with brown, sun-bronzed skin steps out from his sod brick house and looks to the running creek in the distance. With a Spencer rifle held in the crook of his arm, the man stands in front of the doorway and carefully studies the quiet terrain. Adjusting the wide brim of his beaver-felt hat to shade his eyes from the sun, he surveys the scrubby line of trees and tall grasses along the shoreline. His gaze travels to the craggy, rock bluff that hangs high over the far side of the waterway.

A puff of white gun smoke rises from near the water's edge and, as the distant shot rings out, the man at the cabin ducks back inside for cover. He shoulders the Spencer rifle, takes quick aim toward the river and fires-off a round. Suddenly, multiple blasts of gunfire erupt from concealed positions near the creek. Taking cover in the sod house, the man defends his home, returning fire with patient accuracy.

~*~

Traveling from the rolling plains in the east, a tall horseback figure, wearing a fringed, buckskin shirt and an aged cavalry hat, rides with a scruffy canine trotting alongside. Behind them, two youngsters, seated astride captured Indian ponies, follow. Silently observing their surroundings, the small group rides at an unhurried pace.

In the lead, former U.S. cavalry scout, Holton Lang, holds up his mount. Perceptively, he notices the ears of his horse twitch and then perk toward a faraway sound. He turns his head into the breeze and listens. Holton's keen ear can barely make out the distant pop of gunfire. As the pair of younger men ride up beside him, Holton turns to the eldest of the two. "Do ya hear that, boy?"

Jules Ward stops his mount, hears the gunshots, and instinctively puts his hand to the grip of the fancily engraved Colt revolver holstered at his hip. He looks up at Holton. "Thought it might be thunder, but then the wind changed…"

As the youngest of them stops his horse beside Jules, Holton glances at the boy. Thinking on his obligation to protect both boys, he utters, "It was gunshots, alright."

With his hand still resting on the handle of his pistol, Jules scans the terrain around them. "Could be trouble…"

Del Rio Hondo

Holton stares off at the distant hills. "Not for us…"

Jules studies Holton a moment, then looks to the boy, William Parker, mounted on the pony next to him. He turns his gaze to where the shots came from, and stares toward the horizon. "Could be, someone is in trouble…"

Holton replies, "Could be…"

"We gonna do something?"

Holding his mount back, Holton considers their options. The dog barks a warning, and the horses tense-up in anticipation, when there is another volley of faraway gunshots. Looking over to his young companions, Holton reluctantly reaches down and draws out his rifle from the saddle scabbard. Positioning the butt-plate of the rifle stock against his thigh, barrel tilted skyward, he addresses them. "You both stay here. I'll check it out."

Before a word can be uttered from them in protest, Holton spurs his mount and charges ahead, and the eager canine follows. As he leaves, Jules glances at the younger boy next to him while drawing out his own fancy six-shooter pistol. In a huff, he mutters, "He thinks he can leave me behind…"

Beside him, the boy, William, chokes-up on his reins, getting ready to ride. "If *you* go, I'll *follow* you."

Jules takes a moment to watch Holton and the dog ride out of sight over a distant hill, before looking back at William. "Yeah, that's what I figured…" With a kick of his boot heels, his pony leaps forward. "Heeyaww!! Let's go!"

3

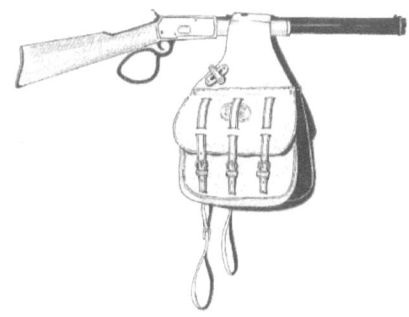

Chapter 2

Black-powder smoke wafts through the air, as gunshots are exchanged between the sod house and the shooters creek-side. One of the ambushers, positioned by a scrubby oak at water's edge, catches a bullet, and tumbles backward. Writhing in pain, his movements gradually slow and, finally, stop. After another brief burst of gunfire, the skirmish comes to a quiet standstill.

As the puffs of gunsmoke drift away in the breeze, the man crouched inside the doorway of the sod house reloads his Spencer rifle through the end of the stock. When he finishes, he cocks the hammer back in a series of clicks, takes careful aim, and waits. Down at the water's edge, a man moves through the tall grass, until a blast of a rifle comes from inside the cabin. Shots are exchanged, and the violent eruption of gunfire commences again.

~*~

Coming over the horizon, rifle in hand, Holton holds-up his mount, looks back, and waits for the two boys to catch up. He looks to the younger boy, William, then turns to Jules, before grumbling, "I thought I told you both to stay put…"

Twirling the fancy pistol on his forefinger, Jules grins. "We come to help."

"Figured as much…"

Jules looks at Holton, as he tilts his head over to the younger boy next to him. "He don't own a shooter, but having numbers on our side might favor us some."

Holton reaches across with his left hand to his sidearm, draws it from the holster and hands it to Jules. "He's your responsibility, so make sure he knows how to use it safely."

Nudging his Indian pony sideways, closer to Holton, Jules takes the pistol and then turns to address the young boy. "Ever used one of these?" William stares and nods his head without uttering a word. Jules continues, "Keep it close, and don't shoot unless you're sure you have to."

The boy takes the offered pistol and holds it on his lap. "Okay… I'll follow you."

Jules glances at Holton, whose attention is on the exchange of gunfire ahead of them, and then instructs further. "Be sure not to cock it without aiming. And, don't shoot that thing with one of us in front of you."

The boy clutches the gun and nods. "Yes, sir…"

Del Rio Hondo

Holton waits until he thinks Jules is finished and offers, "You ready for this?"

As his pony prances and skitters sideways, Jules gives another showy twirl of his pistol and then points it skyward. "As yer ol' pal, Bear, would oft'n say, *I was born ready!*"

Dog lets out a bark and hunkers down, ready to bolt. Jules gives a sharp kick of his heels, offers his mount free rein and charges ahead. After exchanging a quick look with young William, Holton points his rifle down toward the cabin by the creek and proclaims, "Alright, kiddo... *Let's go!*"

~*~

As the riders charge down the slope toward the conflict, the gunfire ceases. Seeing the unexpected reinforcements, the men at the creek dash from cover and head for where their horses are tied in a gully. Riding hard as he veers for the cabin, Holton overtakes Jules and yells, "Git alongside that stack of wood by the barn and use it for cover!" With William following, Jules turns his pony and rides toward the outbuilding.

Bringing his horse to a skidding stop in front of the cabin, Holton glances inside at the man with the Spencer rifle. "Hallo the house. Don't shoot!" Looking to the men mounting their horses at the creek, he utters, "We're here to help..."

The man, Francisco Garcia, lowers the aim of his rifle, pokes his head out from the open doorway, and calls to the rider outside. "Who's side you on, muchacho?"

"Yer's, I s'pose!"

7

He waves Holton aside, as he lifts his rifle to aim beyond the visitor to the men at the creek. "You best take cover then. Them bandito vaqueros have come 'ere to kill me."

Spotting the dead man by the trees, Holton turns his attention to the four horseback men charging up from the gully. Turning his mount to face the approaching riders, he brings his rifle to his shoulder and takes aim.

The riders fire their guns as they charge, and several bullets rip past Holton to smack into the cabin behind him. When Holton and Francisco shoot simultaneously, one of the assailants tumbles and falls from the saddle. Holding their fire, the other riders reign-up their mounts.

The one in the lead lowers his weapon and calls out. "Hey there...! This ain't yer fight!"

Holton grips a fistful of reins in one hand and twirl-cocks his lever-action rifle with the other. "No, sir. Is it yourn?"

"We're jest doin' our job."

Holton glances down at Francisco in the doorway and then notices the family behind him in the cabin. Turning back to the riders, he declares, "You best be ready to be kilt for the fella who pays yer wages."

The flummoxed attackers look to their dead companion, exchange glances between them, and then turn their horses to ride off. One of them grabs the halter of the loose saddle-mount, while the others ride toward the creek where another horse roams free.

Chapter 3

As the riders depart, Francisco comes out to stand in front of the cabin. His features brighten, and he flashes a grin at Holton. "Muchas gracias, Señor…"

"De nada."

Francisco uncocks the hammer of his rifle. "They will surely come back again. By mistake, I killed one of them by the creek before you arrived, and the man on the horse was only to get a warning shot."

Still mounted, Holton looks, unremorsefully, to the dead man by the trees and the other one that fell from horseback. "Too bad for him... My warning shot was for them others."

Leaning his weapon against the cabin, Francisco looks toward the dead bodies. "Now, there are men to be buried."

Holton rests his rifle across his lap, and then looks to Jules and William leading their horses over from the woodpile. "Always figured, I'd rather be the one to do the buryin' than the other way 'round."

Watching the boys approach, Francisco takes note of their age. He sees Jules holster his pistol and observes how delicately William carries his handgun. Nodding to them both, he smiles and offers, "I thank all of you for coming to my aid."

Jules steps up and moves his gaze across the homestead. "That was over quick."

The smile falls from Francisco's face, and he shakes his head sadly. "No, it is not over. Unfortunately, it has been coming for a long time."

"What did they want?"

"Everything I have..."

Leading his horse, Jules stops next to Holton in front of the cabin and sees someone peeking out from the dark window. "Your family?"

"Yes... And, my land..."

Turning his horse, Holton peers into the small cabin. "You should take your family and leave here."

Francisco looks at Holton and then over to the boys. "Without my land, I would not be able to feed my family, and then where would we be?"

Jules tilts his head. "You'd die for the land?"

Del Rio Hondo

With the barrel of his rifle, Holton points in the direction of the two dead men. "They died for less..."

Francisco spits to the side and then peers behind into the cabin. "Yes... They only come here because they are paid for the task of getting us away from here." When he motions to his family, a dark-haired woman and a teenaged daughter step out. "We stay, because we cannot afford to leave."

As a show of respect for the women, Holton swings a leg over the saddle and steps down from his horse. "Was there no offer to pay for your land?"

"There was a proposal once, but not one we would want to accept. Where would we be without the land?"

Tipping his hat to the womenfolk, Holton murmurs, "Still alive..."

"We are alive in our home. Where would we start over, and who says it would not happen the same way again?"

Jules turns and hands the reins of his horse to William, who is standing quietly behind him. Looking the family over, he offers, "You could go back to Mexico."

Francisco narrows an eye and makes an odd face at Jules. "Do I look like a *Mexican* to you?"

Taken aback, Jules looks at Holton and gets no help. Then, he looks back to Francisco. "Uh, yes, you *do*..."

"I am *Spanish*." He walks over to his family and puts his arm around his wife and daughter. "Forgive me for not introducing myself. I am Francisco Garcia, and this is my wife, Leticia, and my daughter, Alejandra."

Holton tucks his rifle under his arm and removes his hat. "Pleased to make yer acquaintance. I am Holton Lang." Turning to the boys, he gestures for them to remove their hats as well. "This is my young friend, Jules Ward, and his friend, William."

Jules studies the dark-featured woman and then the girl, about his own age and much fairer complected, like her father. Aloud, he wonders, "Y'all are *Spanish*…?"

Francisco flashes a big smile, looks fondly at his family, and shakes his head. "No… My wife is Mexican."

Jules looks at Alejandra and then back to her father. "What does that make your daughter?"

He stares at Jules in a peculiar way, proudly declaring, "She is an American."

Amused, Holton smiles to himself and takes his horse by the reins to lead it away. "Now that everyone knows each other, we still have some men that need buryin'."

Francisco casts a glance to his wife, and when she nods he turns back to the three visitors. "We have very little food, but we would like to share a meal, if you will eat with us."

Holton can see that the two boys are eager to stay. Noticing the trickle of wood-smoke coming from the chimney and the smell of food on the cookfire, he nods. "We could eat."

Francisco steps up to take the halter of Holton's horse. "That is good. I will care for the needs of your animals first. Then, we can tend to the dead."

12

Del Rio Hondo

Francisco motions for the boys to follow him, as he leads Holton's horse toward the barn and corral. Standing alone, Holton watches the wife and daughter go back into the cabin to prepare the meal. A pang of nostalgia washes over him, as he thinks back to what little he knew of a traditional family, growing up first at a remote military outpost and then in an Apache village. Holton's gaze drifts from the cabin to the barn, and then to the pair of bodies sprawled lifeless, who will never see their families again.

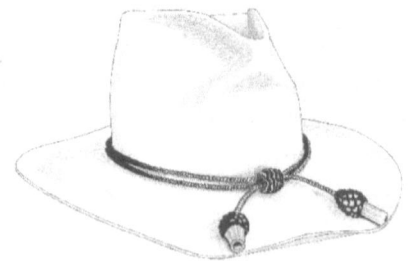

Chapter 4

Sitting in the shade of the veranda, next to the sod house, Holton and the boys finish their meal. Francisco sits with his back leaning on the dirt wall and his Spencer rifle propped up within easy reach. He rubs a finger across the front of his teeth. "My wife is a very good cook, no?"

Jules replies, "Yes! And, just as good as Holton..." Chewing, Holton wipes his mouth and nods to the womenfolk.

Impressed, the Spaniard smiles and looks at Holton. "You are a good cook, Señor?"

"I make do..."

At the end of the table, William, finished with his meal, silently watches everyone. Alejandra takes his empty plate and pats the young boy on the shoulder. "Would you like more?"

"No, ma'am… Thank you."

She grins at his use of *ma'am* for her and gamely replies, "Do you think of me as an old woman? I am only a few years older than you, so you may call me Alejandra, if you'd like."

Softly, he offers, "Okay… Thank you."

She gathers a few more of their dishes and follows her mother back into the cabin. Jules waits for them both to go inside and then leans forward on the table. He asks politely, "Have you lived here a long time?"

Francisco lets his gaze leisurely drift to the small barn then all around at his modest homestead. "I bought this land, and we have lived here since before my daughter was born." He pats the sod-brick wall behind him. "I built the house first, while I made the adobe blocks for my barn."

A cool breeze passes under the veranda, as Jules follows Francisco's survey of the spread. "How long have these other people been wanting your land?"

Francisco sips from a hollowed gourd cup and shrugs. "People always seem to want what someone else already has. The men who build and own the railroad want this water for the new route they have coming through."

Holton finishes his plate and scoots it across the table. "Why don't they jest acquire some land upstream from you?"

15

Eric H. Heisner

Turning his head, Francisco glances toward the creek and eyes the tall trees that line the bank and the cliff beyond. His gaze drifts and then lingers on the pair of fresh graves. "Here on my land, the water comes up from the ground. It is a special place that provides for my crops, my family, and cattle."

Holton considers the conflict and nods understandingly. "If there's a profit to be made, and big business is behind it, they won't stop until you're dead or moved off."

Francisco leans forward to put his elbows on the table and peers inside at his wife and daughter. He turns to Holton. "My friend, I am afraid you are right. But, I will do my best."

Listening, Jules clenches his fists in anger. "Out here, beyond the settlements, being disadvantaged in numbers doesn't mean the end of it. You can still fight."

Surmising that the young man is getting his dander up for a fight that isn't his, Holton is concerned. "Ask the Indians how that is working for *them*."

Understanding Holton's point, Jules turns back to Francisco. "What about the law? *They* should be on your side."

"There is a town marshal in Big Spring, and a sheriff that covers the county… Sadly, they are but two men who would rather not get involved."

Not to be discouraged easily, Jules thinks for a moment, then responds, "What about the Texas Rangers?"

Francisco shrugs. "The Rangers of Tejas have not been known to come to the aid of those with a darker shade of skin. "There's a camp of them near Colorado City, but we cannot go, for if we leave here, they will not let us return."

Coming out from the cabin, Leticia and Alejandra gather the remainder of the meal dishes. Watching them, Jules can't help but let his attentions linger on the teenage daughter. Catching his gaze, she peeks over at him and smiles.

After the women leave and most of the blush fades from his cheeks, Jules puts his hand on the table. "We could help."

Holton turns to him. "We already *did*…"

"No… I mean, we could stay to help defend this place, or ride to the ranger camp to plead their case."

Francisco sighs and leans his chair back against the wall. "Thank you, hijo, but it is our fight, and we cannot pay for an extra hand to help us."

Jules leans further over the table and whispers to him, "Can you at least *feed* us while we're here?"

Holton coughs and gives Jules a reprimanding glare. "Thought we were bound for places north?"

Jules returns the chiding look with a stare of his own. "Those mountains up in Colorado sure ain't going anywhere, and this family needs our help."

"It's not our place to interfere."

"Who says it's not?"

Holton makes an obvious gesture to the recent graves. "Whoever sent those men will be sendin' others, and if we were to stay, there could be a whole lot more killin'."

Challenging him, Jules scoots his chair to sit upright. "Since when is Holton Lang afraid of a fight?"

Taking a deep breath, Holton keeps his composure in front of their host. Glancing to the boy at the end of the table, he replies, "What about young William, here?"

Jules turns to the boy. "He can decide for himself."

The younger boy gazes around at the sparse homestead and turns to catch a glimpse of the women cleaning up inside. He replies simply. "I'll follow you."

Disappointed, Holton averts his gaze, shaking his head. He looks to Francisco, who shrugs. Then, he addresses Jules. "How 'bout we get some rest and talk it over in the morning."

Rising from his seat, Francisco claps his hands together. "That's a fine idea." He grabs his rifle and cradles it on his arm. "I would welcome any help, but there is no reward to offer, so I cannot ask you to stay." He waves his hand toward the barn. "Your horses have been tended to, and you are welcome to rest near them for the night."

Holton stands and reaches to where his rifle leans against the table. "Thank you for the meal and your hospitality, but we'll be leavin' on the morrow." Jules shoots him a look and then stands up. Without uttering a word, he turns to William, who obediently gets up to follow him. Holton extends his hand to Francisco, and they shake. "We'll settle-in for the evening and leave you to your family."

"Buenas noches."

Del Rio Hondo

"And, a good night to you…" Holton tilts his head to the canine sitting nearby and, together, they depart for the barn. Jules watches them go, glances at the window of the sod cabin, and then nods to their host. "Thank you for the fine meal, sir."

"It is the very least we could do to try and repay you for your help today."

"Goodnight."

The Spaniard holds his rifle, while he watches Jules and William follow Holton to the barn. When his wife appears at the cabin window, she suggests, "They are good people."

"Yes… That is what troubles me."

Chapter 5

Early the next morning, Holton gathers his horse and the two ponies, and loops their lead ropes on the upper rail of the fence. Gazing to the western sky, with the sun on the back of his neck, he then turns when Jules comes out of the barn.

Wiping the sleep from his eyes, Jules stares at the three animals lined up along the fence. He looks from the horses to question Holton. "You're leaving?"

"*We're* leavin'."

Jules glances back into the barn where William still rests and then returns his gaze to Holton. "You speaking for us *all*?"

Holton leaves the corral and walks past Jules into the barn to retrieve his saddle tack. Coming back, carrying his rig, he murmurs under his breath to Jules. "Nope…"

"These people need our help."

After hoisting the saddle over the top rail of the corral, Holton separates his horse blanket and shakes it out. He looks at Jules through the fence rails and brushes his hand on the pad. "They were doin' fine before we came and will continue after."

"But, for how long?"

After laying the saddle blanket across his horse's back, Holton smooths it out with his hand. He returns to the fence, takes his saddle off the rail and places it on the animal's back. Letting the stirrups and cinch strap dangle, he glances back to Jules on the other side of the fence. "I can't tell you how to live, but this fight ain't yours."

"If we don't stay to help, who will?"

Stepping around his horse, Holton inspects the rigging and then fastens the cinch. Contemplating his next words, he straightens up, looks around and takes a deep breath. "Wherever you might look, there's *always* some fight to be had. You will have to decide for yerself if it's a thing worthy of livin' or dyin' for."

Half-asleep, with straw stuck in his hair, William emerges from the barn. He sees the two of them faced-off on opposite sides of the corral fence and asks, "Are we leavin'?"

Under his mentor's silent stare, Jules finally utters, "*Holton* is movin' on." Through the fence, they watch as Holton resumes the task of saddling and then slips the horse's bit and headstall on. Jules speaks for the

Del Rio Hondo

benefit of the boy now standing beside him. "Mister Lang has *other* places he wants to be." He turns to William and asks, "How 'bout *you?*"

Looking from Jules to Holton and then back again, the youngster is confused as to which route to take. Jules stands his ground, stating, "I'll be staying *here,* as long as I'm needed."

William looks again to Holton standing beside his horse, and then back at Jules. "I'll follow you."

Holton nods his consent and looks over his saddle to the pair of Indian ponies tethered beside his mount. "I'll turn your animals loose in the corral, then."

Jules remains stoic. "You were the one to catch them ponies for us. They rightfully belong to you."

Suppressing his paternal notions and trying to keep his tone firm, Holton looks back to Jules. "I got no use for 'em. They're yours now." Slipping a boot into the stirrup, Holton steps up and swings a leg over the saddle. Shifting in his seat, he looks down at the two boys. "Good luck to the both of you." He reaches over to the ponies and unties the ropes from around their necks. The animals back away from the fence rail and wander off into the corral.

As Holton exits the corral, Jules swings the gate closed and secures it behind him. "Where're ya headed?"

Holton studies the boys and then casts his gaze north. "Still would like to see that mountain country in Colorado…"

"Then, back to the ranch in Arizona…?"

"Yaugh… And yer still welcome back there anytime. That goes for the both of ya."

Jules nods solemnly. "It was great riding with you again, Holton Lang."

Looking at them fondly, jaw clenched, Holton murmurs, "Yes... Yes, it was." He looks over at Dog, sitting where the corral connects to the corner of the barn. "C'mon, Dog..." Holton turns his horse to leave, and then stops to look back. Dog sits up and looks tentatively between Jules and Holton, obviously conflicted on which path to choose. Holton lets out a snort and a chuckle. "It's fine, Dog... You do what you want." Nudging the rowels of his spurs to his horse's belly, Holton rides over to the sod cabin.

Francisco steps outside. Jules watches, as Holton exchanges a few words with the man and then reaches down to shake his hand. Briefly looking back at the boys, Holton gives a farewell wave and then turns his horse to the north-west. Kicking to a lope, the westerner rides away over the far hillside, opposite the direction from which they had come the day prior.

Chapter 6

Holton draws his rifle from the saddle scabbard and dismounts alongside a swiftly running stream. He lets his horse drink and then bends down to fill his canteen. Catching his watery reflection in the current, he gets a pang of loneliness at the thought of leaving Jules and the young boy behind. Speaking to his mirrored image flowing past, he grumbles. "Some loner *you* are..." Suddenly, he catches a glimpse of someone on the hill behind him, raising a rifle and taking aim. Before he can turn, the snap of a gunshot breaks the silence.

As Holton jumps to his feet and pivots, the sharp bite of a bullet tears through his side. The impact pushes him back to the water, and the last thing he sees before plunging into the stream is two others, with rifles, coming up alongside the first.

~*~

Back at the homestead, Jules hauls an armful of chopped firewood to the depleted stacks alongside the cabin. Turning, he sees Francisco riding in. Jules watches as the experienced rider veers toward the barn, dismounts and ties his horse at the corral. Keeping his rifle handy, Francisco unsaddles his mount, rubs it down well, and sets it loose inside the fenced enclosure. Noticing Jules stacking the wood, the rancher walks toward the young man. "Muchas gracias, Señor Ward."

Jules finishes with his pile. "It's the least I can do."

Francisco looks to the other side of the cabin and sees his daughter playing with William in the shade of the veranda. "It's good that I was able to go out today to check on my cattle. In fear for my family, I have not ventured far."

Turning from the woodpile, Jules looks to the coiled, rawhide riata that Francisco has slung over his left shoulder. "How many cows do you have?"

The Spaniard pauses and smiles pleasantly. "Ahh, that is like asking a man how much dinero he has in his pocket." Embarrassed, Jules looks away and watches the two others laughing and playing. Francisco pats Jules on the shoulder, "Have you worked cattle before?"

Jules turns to him and shakes his head. "No, sir..."

Del Rio Hondo

"Do you know how to use a rope?"

Self-conscious, Jules rests his hand on the grip of his holstered revolver. "No, but I know how to shoot *this*."

With his warm and friendly way of laughing, Francisco unslings the coil of braided leather rope from his shoulder. "Your marksmanship will not impress my animals much. Come... I will show you." He hands Jules the rope, and they walk toward the corral. "Perhaps, one day, you will trade your pistola for a fine riata."

Jules looks down at the finely braided strands of leather in his hand. "Perhaps..."

The rancher smiles. "Then, you will be a vaquero."

~*~

The late day sun looms close to the horizon, as Holton pulls himself from the cold current. Soaked, and still clutching his rifle, he crawls onto the shore. Peering down at his wounded side, he winces and falls to the ground.

Laid out in the tall grass, Holton's chest heaves for breath, as the water drips from him. Staring up to the heavens, he finally catches his air, and his body warms as he drifts off.

~*~

William helps Alejandra place table settings for their next meal. With admiring eyes, he looks to her like one would an older sister. They both stop to watch, as her father gives Jules a lesson in using a rope on a tall fence post on the corral.

Eric H. Heisner

While twirling the rope over his head, Francisco does a fancy flick of his wrist and sends the leather loop floating through the air, as if it was an extension of his own arm. When it lays over the post, he flicks the line again, and the loop comes off just as gracefully as when it had landed. He winds up the length of rope and hands it to Jules.

Clutching the coiled riata in one hand, Jules carefully makes a giant loop and then twirls it over his head a few times. He spins the rope fast enough that it makes a whizzing noise and then tosses it. The loop ungracefully slams into the fence post and slides to the ground. Determined to master this seemingly simple task, Jules glances at his instructor, gathers the rope, and tries again. And, again... And, again...

Chapter 7

Sitting around a campfire, three laughing cowboys share a bottle of whiskey. One of them throws a wet cavalry hat across the small fire to another cowboy. "Still cain't believe that shot... Got 'im on the spin."

The cowboy seated across from him picks up the sodden hat and looks it over. "Heck... If you hadn't a'jumped the gun, we would've *all* had a shot."

As the one with the hat tosses it aside, the last cowboy takes a drink and looks to his partners. "Damn the both of ya. All we got fer our trouble was a bronco horse and a durned hat. I'd have liked to git that *rifle* of his."

Eric H. Heisner

The first cowboy reaches out for the bottle of whiskey. "In the mornin', we can ride the stream to find the body."

"I doubt he'll still have a grip on that gun."

"Ya'd think he'd a'dropped it where he hit the water…"

The cowboy that had Holton's hat shakes his head. "Nope… I looked fer it, and it warn't there."

Well, it cain't be far, and we'll find it tomorrow."

One of them leans over and picks up Holton's hat to re-examine its age-worn felt and dirty cavalry cords. "I wonder who that feller was…"

The man opposite him spits into the fire. "All I figger is, he stepped in our business, kilt one of our'n, 'n had it comin'." He takes a swig, corks the bottle, and tosses it to the cowboy holding the hat. Without a sound, Holton steps into the light and swings the butt of his rifle up alongside the man's head. The walnut stock cracks against his skull, knocking a dribble of whiskey from his lips and knocking him unconscious.

Still dripping-wet, and with blood staining his side, Holton aims the rifle at them on the other side of the campfire. "Don't move, or I'll burn you down…" The wide-eyed cowboy freezes in the flickering firelight, still holding both the whiskey bottle and Holton's hat. The cowboy beside him reaches for his pistol and draws. A shot flashes, and the man with the gun in his hand tumbles to the ground. Levering another round into the chamber, Holton turns his aim to the remaining cowboy. "There's always one in the group who has to test it."

Del Rio Hondo

The cowboy lets the hat and whiskey bottle fall and raises his hands. "You gonna kill me, too?"

Holton glances down at the man he just knocked unconscious. "He ain't dead..." Then his gaze travels to the man he just shot. "And, *he* was well-warned."

The cowboy looks to his fallen comrades and then back at Holton. "Who *are* you...?"

"Jest a fella passin' through..."

The cowboy stares at the spot of blood on Holton's side. "Ya hurt bad?"

Touching his wound, Holton mutters, "Been worse-off, 'nd not as bad-off as some..." Standing in the glow of the fire, Holton motions with the tip of his rifle at the cowboy's gun. "Unbuckle that holster belt and scoot back away from it." Eagerly complying, the cowboy takes off his gun and eases back next to his saddle gear.

Holton steps over the fire and grabs the whiskey bottle. With wet hair matted against his forehead, he puts the bottle to his lips and takes a long swallow. Then, the hand gripping the bottle lifts the side of his shirt and pours the rest of the whiskey over his bloody wound. The cowboy, watching carefully, notices that the aim of Holton's rifle never waivers.

"Looks like a real bad one... Yer gonna need a doctor." This causes Holton to glare at the man, as he lets his buckskin shirt fall back over his wound. With a hint of a cunning smile, the cowboy remarks, "In that condition, I don't think you'll make it far..."

Holton sets the bottle down and grabs his hat. "Cowboy, you'd be surprised..." In obvious pain, he slowly puts his hat on and squats with the rifle rested across his lap.

The cowboy looks to his dead companion and warns, "Killin' more of ours won't be treated lightly."

Grabbing hold of the empty bottle, Holton stands. "Takin' a man's life shouldn't *ever* be treated lightly."

"There's a lot more of us that'll come after you."

Taking a step forward, Holton looms over the cowboy. "Not tonight..." As the intimidated cowboy stares up at him, Holton gestures to the side. When the cowboy turns to look, Holton swings the bottle hard, smashing it against the back of the man's head. The glass shatters, and the cowboy slumps over the top of his gear. Holton drops the neck of the broken bottle and surveys the campsite. Finally, he brushes back a wet strand of hair and takes a deep, soothing breath.

Chapter 8

In the morning sunshine, Jules, with little success, resumes his practice with the lariat. After saying goodbye to his wife and daughter, Francisco rides over from the cabin and leans on his saddle horn to watch. He scratches his chin and offers kindly, "I see you practice very much."

Jules turns to him, recoiling the rope after another miss. "Yeah... Am I getting any better?"

"No."

Frustrated, Jules forms another loop and then whirls it around his head several times. He tosses the rope, nearly laying it over the post, but misses. "*Damn...*"

Del Rio Hondo

Sitting up straight in the saddle, Francisco chuckles. "Señor, today I need my rope, and you need to rest your arm."

Jules winds up the riata and walks over to the rancher. "I'll practice more when you return tonight."

Francisco takes the rope and nods. "Perhaps we can get Leticia to braid you a riata of your own."

"Really?"

"With two young muchachos helping her with chores, she might find some extra time."

Just waking, William, with straw in his hair, emerges from the barn. "I would like one, too."

The rider looks at the sleepy young boy and laughs. "You must get up much earlier to catch the day. And, for you, pequeño, it would be a *small* rope. To be used on goats…"

Watching the skilled vaquero recoil the rope to his liking, Jules offers, "We'll watch over things here."

Francisco loops the leather riata over his saddle horn. "Muchas gracias. If there is trouble, fire two shots with your pistola, and I will come with haste." He gives a wave, clenches his thighs against the horse's sides and rides away at a lope. Jules and William watch, until he's out of sight.

Alejandra steps out of the cabin and into the sunshine. Brushing her dark hair in the morning light, she glances over. When Jules sees her, he feels a pang of unfamiliar emotions, much different from the feelings of love he had for his sisters. He looks to William and pulls a piece of straw from his hair. "C'mon, boy. We got chores to do." William shrugs amicably, runs his fingers through his hair to pull out the rest of the straw and then follows.

~*~

Holton, laying back against one of the cowboys' saddle rigs, slowly wakes. Blinking away the sleep, he looks across the smoldering remains of the campfire to the two men lying on their sides with their hands and feet tightly bound together. Holton sits up and adjusts his hat. Mostly dried out from his time in the water, he still appears very much worse for wear. "Mornin', fellas."

Silent, the trussed-up cowboys stare across the fire's ashes at their wounded captor. Wincing, Holton leans over and searches through a cloth sack taken from one of the saddlebags. He finds some hard tack and breaks-off a bite. Chewing slowly, he studies his prisoners. "What outfit you from?"

Without offering a word of reply, they continue to glare at Holton, as he makes himself breakfast from their supplies. He takes a drink from one of their canteens and then glances at the horses tied nearby. "I guess I can check the brands on your animals and take ya both to the local law."

One of the cowboys shifts from his side and grumbles, "You do that... And, see what happens."

Interested, Holton snaps-off another bite and thinks. "Maybe, instead of takin' you home, I'll take ya over to the next county west 'fore ridin' you in."

"Don't matter. They'll come fer us 'fore long."

"Who?"

"We work for the rich fella that owns the local

railroad, and we have the law on our side. When we don't turn up, they'll send more of us out to find out why."

When finished with his breakfast, Holton sits quietly thinking. Finally, he climbs to his feet, flinching in pain from the effort. He looks out to the horizon and then to where the horses are tied. He counts four of them, including his own. Spotting his own saddle tack, he steps over to it and lifts it up, trying not to irritate his wound. "I'm obliged to ya both for holding my horse." The bound men crane their necks to watch, as Holton goes over to the hitching line to saddle his mount. When he comes back, they watch him sort through the saddle pouches and pack gear, taking their ammunition and supplies. Finding a cotton shirt in one of the saddlebags, he tears off a long strip of fabric to use as a bandage. He glances over at the cowboys. "I don't suppose you fellas mind me helpin' myself?"

Holton grimaces in pain, as he lifts the side of his leather shirt and dabs at his blood-crusted wound. One of the cowboys shifts to a sitting position and remarks, "Untie my hands, and I'll help you with that."

The hardened westerner grins at the obvious deception. "Yeah, I'm sure you would..." He finishes applying the bandage and then packs the cowboys' supplies into his own saddle pouches. The men watch Holton load-up his horse, then untie the other animals and remove their halters.

"Don't let our horses loose..."

With rifle in hand, Holton walks back to stand over the pair of bound cowboys. Scanning around, he sees one of the horses trot off for better grazing, while the others linger beside his saddled mount. "You want someone to come to the rescue, don't you? One of them animals will find its way home."

The two men exchange a worried glance. "You're gonna leave us *tied*?"

Holton looks over to their lifeless companion, still in the same position as the night prior. "Being *dead* is the alternative. Hopefully, you'll figure out somethin' 'fore the coyotes come for *that* one."

Cradling his rifle over his arm, Holton goes to his horse. Gingerly, he mounts and turns his steed. As the men struggle against their bindings, one of them cranes his neck to look up and call out. "You *cain't* jest leave us like *this!*"

Holton leans forward to slide his rifle into the scabbard. Then, he turns his back to the morning sun and rides off.

Chapter 9

Holton travels in a westerly direction across the high desert, and looks to the north, where snow-capped mountains peak on the horizon. A lump of bandages bulges under the bloody hole in his buckskin shirt. Sitting loose in the saddle, Holton clutches his side in an attempt to ease the throbbing pain.

Stopping his horse, Holton unfastens his canteen to take a drink. He lifts his shirt, gingerly peels back the bandage and trickles some water over the crusted scab. The surrounding skin is reddish-purple and inflamed. Holton takes a deep breath, turns and looks to his back-trail. Then, to himself, he mutters, "If that dog was along,

I wouldn't have a stiff neck from lookin' back all the time."

Scanning the horizon, Holton looks for sign of anyone following. After a while, his impatient horse paws the ground. Satisfied, Holton taps his heels to the horse's flank and rides on. Glancing to the ground where Dog would usually be at his side, he shakes his head and then carefully scans the terrain ahead. "I got to find a place to hold up a while and let this heal..." Keeping his horse pointed westward, he continues on.

~*~

Beside the adobe barn at the Garcia homestead, several tanned hides are tacked to frames over piles of scraped hair. Francisco's wife, Leticia, uses a butcher's knife to slice long, thin strands from one of them. William, standing to the side of her, holds a stack of the strips across his small, outstretched arms. Cutting another strand, she lays it over the fidgety boy's pile. "*Dios mio...* Stand still, boy, or you will tangle those lines."

William tries to stop twitching and sags his shoulders. "How much longer...? I don't want to do this anymore."

Nearby, Jules uses a sharp, stone scraper to remove the hair from another stretched hide. "Stop yer complaining kid, or I'll have you back on scraper duty." Not wanting to trade jobs, the boy stops wiggling and stands up straight.

From the cabin door, Alejandra watches them work. Sensing her eyes on them, Jules turns to smile at her before continuing with his task. The girl calls out to her mother. "Mama, can William help me with grinding corn for tortillas?"

Leticia sees the young boy's look of excitement at the thought of leaving to help her daughter. Giving a stern look, she shakes her head and then smiles at him. "Yes, William... You may go and..." Before she finishes speaking, the young boy tosses the pile of leather and runs off toward the cabin.

Mouth agape, Leticia looks at the tangled mess on the ground and then at the young boy trotting toward Alejandra. She looks at Jules, who turns his grin away to glance at Dog, sitting in the shade. She stands, speechless, as Jules tries to contain his laughter while resuming his task of scraping.

~*~

Following the embankment of a waterway, Holton comes to a small settlement near the confluence of two rivers. He rides into the adobe village and stops at a shaded ramada, where an old man sits quietly watching him. "Hola, amigo..."

Looking up, the wrinkled, old man displays a toothless grin and squints his eyes against the sunlight. "Hello, gringo... You look none too well."

Holton glimpses down to the dark blood stain at his side. "I've been better..."

Jabbing a crooked finger toward an adobe structure across the way, the old man uses passable English, as he continues. "You need to see the woman that counts the stars." Feeling faint, Holton turns to look at the earthen building. Blinking drips of sweat from his eyes, he has a vision of his dead Apache wife standing in the doorway. He tries to utter words of greeting, but they won't come. When he blinks his eyes closed and opens them again, she is gone. He turns back to the old man, who continues to offer his gummy smile. "Gringo, you should go. Sooner than later..."

Holton bows his head, takes a breath, glances back to the building one more time and then starts to step from his horse. At the twisting of his torso, a wave of pain sweeps through him, and he blacks out. With a thud, he falls to the ground.

For a moment, the old Mexican stares at the motionless figure lying next to the horse. Then, slowly, he climbs to his feet. He shuffles nearer and stands over Holton. Taking the reins, he turns to lead the horse away. "Yes, gringo... You rest a while, and I will tend to your   animal."

Chapter 10

Waking to the smell of wood smoke and food cooking, Holton looks up at the thatched ceiling of a large room. He tries to roll over, but can't, as his shoulders are strapped down. Scanning his surroundings, he finds himself in a primitive, adobe-reinforced shelter, where a grey-haired woman works near a brick fireplace. "Hello...?" When the old woman turns to stare at Holton, he asks, "Where *am* I?" She doesn't answer. Straining against his bindings, he utters, "Why am I tied...?" She lowers her gaze and continues to prepare food.

When he reaches a hand up in an attempt to free himself from the straps, the woman states, "If you shift around too much, it will only bleed more." He stops and touches his side. It feels numb where the bullet exited, and he can feel a bandage packed with plant material.

"Did you bandage me…? How did I get here?"

She stirs her pot, lifts the spoon, and smells the contents. "*They* brought you." She tilts her head to where several children curiously peer at Holton from the open doorway.

"Why?"

Finished with her stirring, the old woman stands and shuffles to his bedside. She inspects the bandaged wound and pulls one of the leather thongs to release her patient's shoulder. "I am called Cielo. They bring all sorts of injured creatures for me to heal." Holton moves, and he tests his ability to get up. "You may sit up. Slowly… So you do not undo all of my work." She helps him to lift his torso and tucks a wadded blanket behind him for comfort.

Looking around the room, he notices that he is in the only bed and that his buckskin shirt is draped over the back of a cane-back chair. "How long have I been here?"

"Not long…"

He studies her dark, wrinkled features. "Who are you?"

"I told you… I am Cielo."

He nods and considers the bareness of the earthen room. "And, you're a healer?"

"I am the woman who watches the stars."

"What do you see in *them*?"

"I try to understand what they *tell* us."

Holton glances outside and notices the bright daylight. Then, he looks into her caring eyes and nods his appreciation. "Thank you for helping me."

"The stars in heaven said you'd be delivered to me... And, a storm would follow."

He looks back to the children watching him and at the clear skies beyond them. "Doesn't *look* like rain..."

"Storms come in *all* manners..."

Resting his hand at his side, Holton notices that his sidearm is missing. He looks around the room to discover his rifle propped in the corner by the chair with his shirt, and his gun belt is on the table nearby. Cielo observes him taking inventory and puts her small hand gently on his shoulder. "Relax, now... The storm may not happen here for many days." Despite her earlier warning, Holton tests his wound and tries to get up. She gives him a scolding look and shifts her hand to rest on his forearm. "If you try to move around too much more, I will have to tie you down again."

"I should be going..."

"Where do you need to go?"

Pausing to catch his breath, he looks at her and replies, "Uh... Well, nowhere, I guess."

"Then, why the hurry?"

Easing back down into the comfort of the small bed, Holton silently muses on his intended path to the mountains of Colorado and then to the ranch in Arizona, where his friends, Alice and Bear, await his return. The thought of going back there in this weakened condition tempers his drive, and he lays his head down. "No hurry..."

Del Rio Hondo

"You would only get sicker and die before you get there, if you were to leave now."

He looks at her curiously. "You read *that* in the stars?"

With a hint of a clever grin, she pats Holton gently on his bandaged side. "I am the one who can put a stop to the spirits that make the wound burn."

A cool breeze passes through the window and sweeps over Holton's clammy skin. Trying to relax, he closes his eyes. As he listens to the curious whispers of the children outside, he drifts off to sleep.

Chapter 11

Jules sits by the barn with Leticia, as she demonstrates how to braid a riata. At the cabin, William helps Alejandra with chores, and Jules can't help but steal the occasional glance their way. Carefully mimicking Leticia's pattern, he works the flat strips of leather together, but eventually drifts back to watching the activity around the cabin.

An attention-grabbing cough brings him back to task. "Hijo, if you don't look at what you do, it will be a poor weave." Jules looks at the leather strands again and tries to follow what the woman shows him. She displays the twisted pattern of lines and waits for him to follow her instruction.

Redoing his braid, Jules curses quietly under his breath. Feeling a disapproving stare from her, he glances up and apologetically mutters, "I'm sorry…"

"I have heard men use language much harder than that." Jules smiles and focuses again on braiding the strips of leather. Watching him keenly, she asks, "Have you ever been married?"

He looks up, surprised. "No…! I'm just a *kid*."

She studies the teenager. "You have an old look in your young eyes…" He looks to his braiding, as she continues. "Ones that have seen things well beyond your years and does not fit with a youthful body such as yours… Do you like girls?"

He continues to braid, concentrating on what he's doing and pretending that he didn't hear the question about girls. When he finally does look up, she is patiently staring at him, waiting for an answer. "Yeah, I guess… I don't know."

Leticia lowers her gaze and proceeds with her weaving. "We never know how long we will be here in this world. Perhaps she will be a good wife for you someday."

Jules looks up and sputters, "I'm not lookin' for a wife."

"Oftentimes, *they* find *you*."

Flushed with embarrassment, Jules watches Leticia braid the leather strands. Unable to find the words, he simply follows her lead. For a long while, he resists the urge to look over at Alejandra. His heart thumps in his chest when he hears her laughing with

Del Rio Hondo

William. Eventually, he realizes that Leticia is focused on her work and sneaks a peak toward the cabin.

~*~

As Jules tends to the farmyard animals, he notices the two Indian ponies in the corral are restless and perking their ears to the distance. Jules stops and turns to scan the horizon. From over a far hillside, about a half dozen riders approach the homestead at a brisk trot.

Jules sprints into the barn, while hollering toward the cabin. 'William… Get the women inside!"

The young boy stops kneading the corn mash and looks up to the approaching riders. Leticia steps outside the doorway, and Alejandra stands watching from the shade of the veranda. William watches Jules come running from the barn, buckling on his gunbelt and holster. Jabbing a finger in their direction, he gestures for them to go inside. "Get in the cabin and stay away from the door and windows!" The boy joins Leticia and Alejandra at the cabin entry, and then they disappear inside.

With his gunbelt fastened, Jules stands watching, as the group of riders slow to a walk and continue their approach. Scanning the horseback men, Jules assesses their weaponry. Each has a rifle tucked in a saddle scabbard, and they all look to be wearing a cartridge belt and holstered pistol. The rider in the lead eyes the cabin briefly, then rides directly toward Jules.

Jules sees eyes peeking from the doorway and calls out, "Stay inside. I'll handle this…"

The riders slowly fan out to stop, six-abreast before Jules. The leader regards the young man before

51

him and offers, "Hello, boy. I'm looking for the man of the house."

Jules returns the stare and replies. "I'll have to do."

A twinkle in the man's steel-grey eyes acknowledges the youngster's bravery. He glances over to the cabin before looking back at Jules. "And, who are you?"

"Who's doin' the askin'?"

Surprised by the brashness, and noticing the fancy pistol on the boy's hip, he straightens himself in the saddle and states, "*I* am *Colonel Jackson Henry* out of *Fort Worth.*"

Jules slowly eyes the other men lined up in front of him. "You're a ways from home."

"Yes… My work here in this part of the state requires it, and I would like to get to business."

"What *is* your business?"

"Unfortunately, it is none of *yours. Mine* is with the *owner* of this piece of land." He looks to the rider on his right, and the man leans over to whisper a name. The colonel sits up, adjusts his coat lapel, and addresses Jules. "We seek to gain an audience with Señor Francisco Garcia."

"You'll have to settle for me."

"And, again, *who* are *you*?"

"I didn't say."

"No, you didn't."

They stare at one another for a while, until Colonel Henry breaks the standoff. "Young sir, I've introduced myself. The polite thing is to return the courtesy."

"What are you a colonel *of*?"

Unsure if he should be irritated or amused with the young man, the colonel gestures to the riders beside him. "These men and the local railroad…"

"Is it a military railroad?"

"I served in the war of northern aggression."

"And, now you oversee aggression on others?"

Angered now, the colonel looks over to the sod cabin. "You tell Garcia to consider this his final warning. Tell him to move off this land within the week, and he can collect what's been offered at the bank in Fort Worth."

"What if he doesn't want to move?"

His patience exhausted, the colonel glares at Jules while nudging his horse forward. Looming over him, he stares down at the boy and speaks in a low voice, so the those behind him and at the house cannot hear. "Then, he can be *buried* here…"

Jules tilts his head toward the creek and the fresh graves. "He won't be alone."

The colonel heaves a breath and sits up in the saddle. "That is a whole other matter to address. Who was it that rode in with you the other day?" The mention of Holton stirs Jules, and the colonel takes notice.

"He ain't here right now."

The colonel smiles. "We know."

Jules tries to understand his deeper meaning and asks, "You've been watching the place?"

Eric H. Heisner

"We know more of what goes on here than you think. Turns out, your riding companion had a run in with our boys and was wounded a few miles west of here. He will be handled soon enough. It's just a matter of time before the sheriff's posse locates him and deals with him properly."

Remaining stoic, Jules stares up at the mounted colonel. "Have you said all you come to say?"

The colonel bows his head and starts to turn his horse. "Tell Señor Garcia that the railroad is coming through, whether he likes it or not. He can leave with his family or be laid to rest under the tracks." Riding past his men, the colonel leans over to the foreman who spoke to him earlier. When he whispers something, the man nods and looks directly at Jules.

Jules sees the rider separate from the colonel and his men and ride toward him. Putting his hand on the handle of his six-gun, Jules stands his ground. Noticing that the approaching man lets his free hand hang just below the gun slung at his hip, Jules waits, readying himself for a fight. Keeping an eye on the hand nearest the holstered sidearm, Jules stares upward at him and confidently states, "I'm not afraid of you..."

Unexpectedly, the man's boot shoots out from the stirrup and catches Jules along the jawline. The strong blow wrenches Jules' head back and tumbles him to the ground. Before Jules can react and draw his gun, the man has his pistol out and aimed at him. "Go ahead. Do it, boy, 'n I'll kill ya..." Jules stops and glares at the mounted figure through tear-glazed eyes. "If ya want to put a name with a face, its Rickter." Twirling his pistol

Del Rio Hondo

back into its holster, Rickter smirks at Jules and glances back to see his employer riding away. He looks back down at the boy and touches the brim of his hat in a salute. "That was your one and only warning. Won't be another..." Rickter spurs his horse hard, jerks it around toward the others and waves them on to follow after the colonel. "Let's go, boys."

Rubbing the tender spot on his jaw, Jules gets to his feet. He looks to the cabin doorway, where William and the two women peek out. Then, he turns to the barn to see the watchful dog sitting in the shadows. "Holton..." Dog's ears push back. He barks and locks his gaze on the boy. Jules gives the canine an approving nod. Pivoting on a hind leg, the scruffy mongrel dashes off to the west.

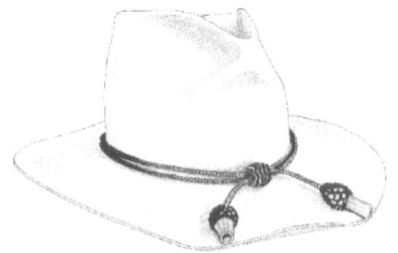

Chapter 12

Sitting up in bed, Holton eats soup from a hand-carved bowl. Fresh bandages are wrapped around his torso and a healthy color has returned to his complexion. He finishes his meal and sets the wooden bowl aside. Rising from the bed, he gingerly touches his wound, heaves a deep breath to keep from fainting and slowly makes his way to the window.

The isolated village is quite peaceful. Sounds of laughter come from kids playing down the street, and the old man continues to sit in the shade across the way. Their gazes meet, and the old man raises a hand in greeting. Holton returns the gesture, wincing from the effort.

Del Rio Hondo

Feeling the presence of someone behind him, Holton turns to see Cielo. He nods to her and says, "I didn't hear you come in."

"There is no place to go very far."

Holton weakly braces himself on the windowsill. "Seems *I've* been far…"

She knows that he wants to be mobile but observes that he still can barely stand. "You feel stronger now, but the mind can deceive the body."

He touches his wound. "When I can see the sky and breathe fresh air, I feel much better."

The old woman sets down her woven basket of freshly picked herbs and moves to prepare something at the fireplace. Holton takes another longing gaze outside, before slowly making his way to sit in a chair pulled up alongside the bed. Cielo diligently observes his every move. Noticing how she watches, he asks, "Do many people live here in this village?"

"Some make a life here."

The sounds of unseen children laughing and playing draw Holton's glance to the open window. "Where are they?"

"The women stay at home, and the men work the fields or take trade goods to the fort."

"A fort nearby… Fort Stanton?" As she prepares food, Cielo nods her head. Holton continues, "The old man and some children are all I've seen."

"They hide away in fear."

A look of surprise crosses Holton's features. "*Of me…?*"

Cielo stops, lifting her eyes to meet the gaze of her guest. "Those with a lighter color of skin, such as yours, have only brought trouble to our village."

"I mean them *no* harm…"

She stares at Holton, then glances out the doorway to the quiet street. "They are simple people with simple thoughts."

Holton relaxes back in the chair, adjusts to ease his pain, and thinks awhile. Finally, he turns his attention back to Cielo, stating, "You mentioned that trouble was coming after me?"

She nods. "It is written in the stars."

"Then, I better be on my way, before it finds me."

Her mischievous gaze turns to lock on his, and she shakes her head. "There is time. It will go much better for us if you are here when they come."

"When *who* comes?"

"The ones I have seen in my visions."

Holton looks to where his rifle is propped beside the bed and his holstered pistol hangs from the gunbelt on a nearby wall-peg. "Do the people in this village have any weapons?" When Cielo shakes her head and looks away, Holton asks, "Why would it be better for me to stay here, if your people can't even defend themselves?"

Silently, Cielo puts her attention to her work. Holton gingerly lifts himself from the chair and makes his way toward the window again. He looks outside. The old man and the sounds of children are gone. Glancing back to the old woman, he mutters, "In my life, I have seen bad things that I wouldn't want to happen here."

Del Rio Hondo

With her eyes cast downward, Cielo offers no response and continues to concentrate on her task.

Feeling weak again, Holton returns to the chair, braces himself on the back, and then has a seat on the edge of the bed. "I will remain for a short time, and then be on my way..." Receiving no reply from the old woman, he lies down to stretch out on the bed. He feels the blood pulsing through his body, as his weakness takes over. He closes his eyes and drifts off to sleep to the sounds of Cielo working in the kitchen.

60

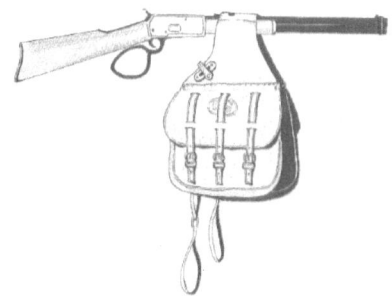

Chapter 13

A rider on a stout, long-haired pony comes over the far hillside and into the small village of Rio Hondo. Slowing to a stiff-legged trot, Ernesto rides past the watchful old man and stops his animal before the old woman's home. "Cielo… Cielo? Where are you, woman?" He turns to gaze down the empty street and then turns back to call into the woman's dwelling. "Where is the gringo?"

Holton, rifle at his side, steps from the shadowed doorway into the bright sunlight, shirtless and with a bandage wrapped around his torso. He takes a good look at Ernesto. "I'm here…"

The Mexican looks to Holton, blurting out his words. "They are coming for you!"

Eric H. Heisner

"Who...?"

"A Tejas sheriff and a posse of men..."

"How many...?"

Ernesto turns and excitedly points. "There are many! Just over those hills, to the east..." Heaving a weary sigh, Holton focuses his gaze in the direction the rider indicates, as the Mexican continues. "They say to me, if you run from here, they will kill many people in the village and then track you down to return you to Tejas."

Clenching his jaw, Holton glances to his rifle in hand. "Tell everyone to keep out of sight, until it's over 'nd done. They only want me." He looks up at Ernesto sitting horseback. "Until I'm gone, there's no need for any of them to fight or even come out of their homes."

Ernesto pats the sweaty neck of his pony and then sits up straight and proud on his worn-out Spanish-style saddle. "Señor, we are not cowards in this village."

"This isn't your fight."

"But, you are our guest."

Holton looks down the vacant street and notices that there is no sound of the children. The message of the approaching posse must have already spread to the villagers. "I'm grateful for your hospitality, but it's time for me to go."

The man, holding his mount from walking away toward the stables, leans down, narrows his eyes at Holton and asks, "You will not fight them?"

"Not if I can help it."

"We are only poor dirt farmers, but we will fight for what is good and right."

Del Rio Hondo

Holton waves Ernesto off. "Go, now... And, tell the others to stay inside until I'm gone."

Crestfallen, Ernesto slides from his mount and leads it toward the corral across the way. Briefly, he glances back to see Holton go back inside the old woman's home.

~*~

In tight formation, the posse comes riding over the hill. As they approach the village, the riders spread out to the width of the street. Positioned at the front, Sheriff Lowe veers over toward the old man watching from where he sits in the shade. "Hola, viejo... Dónde está?"

The old man looks up at the lawman on horseback and then studies each of the men in the posse coming up behind. Finally, he gestures to the building across the street. "There..." The sheriff turns to look across the street, starts that way, and stops when the old man continues. "But, you will not take him."

Hesitating, the sheriff asks, "And, why is that?"

"It is written in the stars."

"By who...?"

The old man responds, "We do not write in the heavens, but she is one who can read what they say."

The sheriff stares at the old man for a moment, then shakes his head in disgust and turns away. "There's always one crazy in town..." He leads the posse to the front of the adobe, and the riders spread out behind him in a wide semi-circle. Laying his rifle over his saddle horn, he is about to bellow, when a figure steps out into the sunlight. Holton wears his blood-stained buckskin shirt and holds his rifle at his side. Sheriff Lowe and the posse assess him, as they position themselves. Then, they survey the adjacent area for any others. Noticing the stain on Holton's shirt, the sheriff surmises, "Guess yer the one we're after…"

"Could be…" Holton keeps his cold stare on the sheriff. "Your quarrel is with *me*, not the folks who live here."

"I'm glad to know my warning got passed along." Sheriff Lowe glances down the empty street of the village. "They seem to get the message."

Holton nods. "They understand white man's ways."

Looking back, the sheriff takes notice of Holton's gun and then moves his own rifle to his lap. "You killed several men back in Texas and have to answer for it."

"Some cain't help but git dead…"

Sheriff Lowe looks at Holton strangely. "Are you sayin' it was self-defense?"

"I wasn't lookin' for a fight."

Everyone sits their horses, waiting, until one of the posse members chimes in. "He shot 'im in *cold blood!*"

Holton studies the man before replying. "I don't remember *you* being there."

"I heard it from them that *was*." The man raises his pistol and aims it at Holton. "Let's hang 'im, or jest shoot 'im here!"

Ignoring the blowhard, Holton looks back to the sheriff. "You're a bit beyond your reach."

"How so…?"

Del Rio Hondo

Holton glances at the badge pinned on the sheriff's vest. "This ain't Texas... *You* ain't *legal* here..."

The sheriff briefly considers his lack of jurisdiction and nods in agreement. "In this territory, I'm jest a concerned citizen. We won't hang ya, official, 'til we git back to Texas."

"I'll ride with you to the military fort."

The sheriff motions for the man pointing the pistol to put it down and then turns back to Holton. "Give us yer weapons, and we'll talk."

Holton evaluates the anxious posse surrounding him. "I'd feel better *keepin'* mine, and *you* puttin' *yours* down."

Clenching his jaw, the sheriff heaves a breath. "Alright... Go git yer horse, and we'll ride to the fort with ya."

When Holton takes a step away from the open doorway, the angry posse member gripes, "To hell with the damn fort... Piss on that!" He raises his gun, hastily aims and fires a shot. Just ahead of Holton, the bullet smacks into the adobe wall.

Instinctively, Holton brings his rifle to his hip and lets-go a return shot. The bullet tears into the man's torso, causing the gunman to fire another shot skyward. He falls out of the saddle and lands with a thud.

His gun still smoking, Holton turns to meet the gaze of the sheriff. Realizing that things have gone awry, he dives for the doorway, just as the lawman raises his rifle and fires. Suddenly, a flurry of gunshots explodes toward the adobe building, sending chunks of earthen brick in every direction.

65

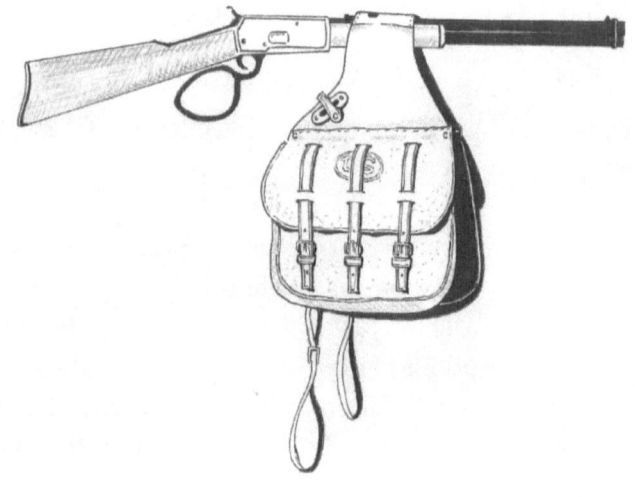

Chapter 14

Holton peers out through a window, as some riders hastily dismount to find cover across the street, and the others scatter. Poking his rifle out the opening, he aims and fires. The bullet cuts the reins of a rider's horse, causing it to rear up and throw the man from the saddle.

A barrage of gunfire unloads on the mudbrick dwelling. Holton hears someone crawling in through the open window behind him and turns to see Ernesto holding a sawed-off shotgun and several boxes of ammunition. "I told you to hide! What the hell are you doin' here?!?"

"I came to help."

"I said to keep clear."

On his belly, crawling beneath the onslaught of bullets coming in through the front window and doorway, Ernesto reaches Holton. "I told you... We are not cowards."

Shots tear through the room. Keeping low against the wall, Holton shakes his head. "Bravery and stupidity are oft'n traveling companions."

"Which one are you?"

"Neither."

"Then, why are you here?"

"Why are *you* here?!?"

Affronted, Ernesto fires his gun and turns to glare at Holton. "You are a *guest* in our village. What a great insult it would be to have you harmed while in our midst."

"Getting dead don't remedy insult."

With a smile, the Mexican man shrugs and reloads. "Death is merely a part of life..."

"It's the *end* part of it..."

"Working in a rocky field all the rest of my days is what I fear more than dying."

As bullets whiz overhead, smashing against the back wall, Holton takes a fresh cartridge from his gunbelt and loads it into the side-gate of his rifle. "Well, damn... Yer here now." He looks across the room to the back wall. "Check and see if they've covered the back window..."

Ernesto places the boxes of cartridges by Holton's side, hunkers down and dashes across the room. He peeks outside and then quickly ducks down, as a bullet rips through the window and hits a cluster of chilli peppers hanging on the wall. Holton watches, as Ernesto hides below the windowsill, then pokes the shotgun's short barrel outside and pulls the trigger. The blast reverberates through the room, and a cloud of burnt powder smoke wafts over them. After looking outside and then back at Holton, Ernesto scurries back, proudly grinning as he reloads the spent shotgun shell. "Sí, Señor. There are several men out there."

"Did you hit anything with that scattergun?"

"Yes! I hit a *lot* of things, and one of them out there has the sting of many tiny bees."

Holton can't help but grin at the Mexican's eagerness. When the frequency of gunfire slows, Holton removes his hat and pokes his head up to scan the street. Most of the posse's horses have fled to the edge of town, and the remaining men are positioned behind woven baskets and low, brick walls. Holton brings his rifle to his shoulder and snaps off a shot.

Howling in pain and holding an injured leg, a man tumbles out from behind a stack of dry goods. Sheriff Lowe pops his head up from behind a wooden barrel and hollers, "You in there… Give it up, and throw out yer guns!"

Holton ducks down, puts his hat back on and replies, "I'll come peaceable, when *you* throw down yours."

A fresh volley of gunfire erupts, and the pair inside the building keep low, as shards of adobe shower down on them. Ernesto wipes dirt from his hair and snorts, "I don't think they are finished quite yet."

Sweeping dust from his shoulder, Holton gives the Mexican a sarcastic look. "*Yeah…? Any ideas…?*"

"If we want to leave, I have both of our horses saddled and waiting for us two houses down."

Surprised, Holton looks at him. "You *do*?"

"With this crowd of gringo desperados, I think we would no want to stick around for very long."

"You figured right. Any ideas how to get to them?"

Ernesto looks toward a wooden cabinet against the wall. "Some of these homes share a wall to save on bricks and heat. Maybe we can get out next door?"

Bullets continue to tear into the room, as Holton crawls across the floor toward the large cabinet. Turning around the corner of a low wall near the fireplace, he sees the feet of the old woman. Over the sound of gunfire, he hisses loudly. "Cielo... It's not safe here. We need to get you out of..." Moving to her, he notices blood on the front of her blouse. With a heavy sigh, he reaches out to her lifeless body. Staring at her resting features, he touches her on the cheek. "I'm sorry..."

Coming behind, Ernesto peers over Holton's shoulder and harshly whispers, "Is the old lady finally dead?"

Surprised at the callousness, Holton looks back at him. "What do you mean, *finally*?"

Ernesto shrugs innocently. "She lived a very long time." He then adds, "When I was a boy growing up in this village, she was a very old woman even back then."

Keeping low, Ernesto crawls to the wooden cabinet and starts to push it aside. Holton helps him scoot it from the wall, and they study the bricks near the dirt floor. The aged adobe is flaky and cracked. "How thick is that wall?"

When Ernesto taps the brick with the butt of his shotgun, it crumbles a bit. "The old woman was muy antigua, but this house she lived in is very much older." He smashes against the wall again and looks over his shoulder to Holton. "Some of these homes were made before my grandparents were born." Ernesto sweeps the crumbled adobe aside and continues to smash at the wall, while Holton keeps watch toward the doors and windows. Eventually, enough bricks are broken loose to create a small opening. Ernesto looks over at Holton and grins. "Señor, we can go now."

Holton looks at the opening. "You go first."

Ernesto pauses, looking at Holton suspiciously. "Hey… Is this a trick to be rid of me?"

Holton levers his rifle, pops up and fires a shot through the window. He picks up a box of ammunition and tosses the other one to Ernesto. "Just do what I say."

Ernesto catches the box, grins enthusiastically and gets on his belly to crawl through the broken-out hole in the wall. After returning another volley of gunfire, Holton turns to see that Ernesto has made it through the wall. Poking his head up again, Holton snaps-off another round and ducks, as multiple gunshots are returned.

Keeping low, he pours the cartridges out of the box, reloads his rifle and then the empty loops on his gunbelt, and then he crawls toward the hole. After a quick glance back to the old woman peacefully at rest under shards of broken pottery, Holton ducks down and scurries through the small opening.

Chapter 15

Holton makes his way through the hole in the broken wall. On the other side, he sees Ernesto, positioned at the back door, and a woman, huddled with her children at the opposite wall. He feels a pang of dread for endangering an innocent family, until Ernesto softly calls out to him. "They are fine, Señor... Worry not. She is my cousin. Hurry! We can go out this way."

Apologetically, Holton glances at them and whispers, "Lo siento..." A boy's eyes light up and, with a wave, he grins. Making his way across the room to the back door, Holton peeks over Ernesto's shoulder. Outside, a man, with his back to them, is watching the rear window of the old woman's home.

Del Rio Hondo

Ernesto raises his scattergun and glances back to Holton. "I shoot him now, and we go...?"

"In the *back*?"

"No...?"

"*No.*"

Ernesto shrugs and lets out a whistle. The man turns around to face them, and Ernesto lets loose with the shotgun. Holton shakes his head in dismay and dashes out the door. "*C'mon, let's git...*"

~*~

Making their way down the alley, Holton and Ernesto get to the saddled horses and mount up. As gunfire continues up the street, they trot to the far end of the village, Holton stops and looks to the man beside him. "Which way to Fort Stanton?"

Ernesto points northwest, opposite from where the riders came in. "About twenty-two miles that way..."

Rifle in hand, Holton holds his horse back. "You ride for the fort and see if you can get some help."

Ernesto looks blankly at Holton. "But, what about *you*?"

"I will try to draw these men away from the village, so no one else gets hurt."

The Mexican notices that Holton's wound is bleeding. Conflicted, he hesitates and holds his mount back. "No, no, no. This plan is not a good one."

"It's what we've got."

Ernesto shakes his head. "Who at the fort will help?"

"Find someone who doesn't like Texans."

Eric H. Heisner

Thinking on it, the Mexican half-nods in agreement. "There is always someone…"

"If that posse thinks soldiers from a fort are on their way, they won't stick around."

Thinking on it more, the Mexican replies, "Maybe I let them *think* I ride for help and then circle around to help you?"

Holton spins his anxious horse around to settle it down. As gunfire continues down the street, he faces Ernesto. "*No…* Go to the fort, tell 'em, and I'll lead these men *away* from here."

Ernesto considers the plan again and shakes his head. "Not a very good idea… I should stay with you."

"Just *do* it!"

Still shaking his head in protest, Ernesto prods his horse and gallops westward. When a dog barks between gunshots, Holton feels a reminiscent chill. "Glad you're not along with me on this one…" Holton watches, as Ernesto finally disappears over the hilltop. Then, rides his horse back toward the center of the village.

~*~

Holton trots down the main street and slows to a walk. Men are still shooting from cover, as he rides toward the old woman's home. Lifting his rifle and putting it to his shoulder, he lines up the sheriff in his gunsights. Then, he raises his aim a bit higher to hit a clay pot, hanging overhead, holding water. The vessel explodes and rains down on the men underneath.

Startled by the seemingly errant gunshot, the shooting suddenly stops, and the men turn to see Holton

Del Rio Hondo

up the street. Several of the men come out of hiding and walk toward him. As the late afternoon sun shines brightly behind him, Holton sits tall in the saddle and gives his big-loop rifle a one-handed twirl-cock. Resting the butt of the rifle on his thigh, he calls out to the sheriff and his posse. "Leave this place now, and I'll let you return to Texas."

Dripping wet, the sheriff steps into the street to face Holton. "Listen, fella… Yer way with numbers ain't so good."

Several more men emerge from cover and lever their rifles. As he counts them, Holton mutters under his breath. "Well, shit…" Suddenly, a yelping dog comes running from the far end of the village. Two men step aside, as the scruffy canine scampers past them and stops beside Holton. Panting heavily, Dog looks up, satisfied. Surprised, Holton looks down at him and remarks, "Well, it's good to see you…" He shakes his head. "But, your timing isn't the best."

Down the street, the sheriff lets out a throaty chuckle. "Give it up now… Or, we'll shoot ya *and* yer ugly dog!"

Bracing himself in the saddle, ignoring the pain of his wound, Holton tightens a fistful of reins and looks down to the canine beside him. "You ready, Dog…?"

The dog rumbles out an affirming growl, hunkers down, and prepares to spring forward. Holton clenches his thighs tight against his mount and slaps the barrel of his rifle across the horse's rump.

"Heeeyaa! Let's go!!!"

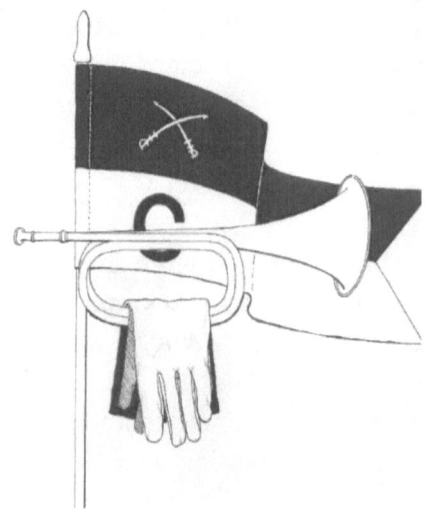

Chapter 16

The men in the street stand, awestruck, as Holton and the growling canine charge toward them. The sheriff raises his rifle, draws a steady bead on Holton and, just as he is about to pull the trigger, hears the distinct bugle charge of the US Cavalry. His men quickly recognize the sound as well, and Sheriff Lowe turns to see them promptly scatter, racing to find their mounts. The sheriff looks back at Holton and the dog and hastily squeezes off his shot. The bullet goes wide, and Lowe jumps back just as Holton gallops past him. One of the other men

Del Rio Hondo

doesn't get out of the way in time. Holton swings his rifle out, catches the man across the shoulder and spins him aside.

As the echoing blast of the bugle gets nearer, Holton stops his horse at the opposite end of the street. He looks to the hills and sees an approaching troop of cavalry with the red and white guidon flag waving high. At the front of the column, Ernesto, on his shaggy-haired mount, waves his floppy hat over his head. To himself, Holton murmurs, "That Mexican can ride like the wind, or that patrol was already nearby…"

Turning back toward the village, Holton sees the posse grabbing for their horses and mounting up. They scatter in every direction other than that of the advancing military. Watching the sheriff's sudden departure, Holton, with Dog at his side, sits waiting for the cavalry to arrive.

Ernesto and the officer-in-charge ride up to Holton, as the rest of the troopers gallop past to occupy the village. Slapping his hat back on his head, Ernesto grins proudly. "Señor…! Señor, see who I have found to help us."

Resting his rifle across his lap, Holton looks at the cavalry officer and recognizes him. "*Captain Fellows…?*"

This chance meeting has the officer just as surprised. "Well, I'll be damned, *Holton Lang*… And, it's *Major* now."

Holton snaps off a salute reminiscent of his days scouting for the military. "Yes, sir."

Eric H. Heisner

Major Fellows gives the former scout a looking over. "Mister Lang, I do have to say, you seem a bit worse for wear. Is that an old wound or a new one?"

Looking at his injury, Holton sees fresh blood running down his pant leg. "I don't mend as good as I once did."

Fellows grins. "But, still find the same sort of troubles." The Major scans the troopers filling the street and concludes that the village is protected from any further aggression. "Appears the excitement is over. On our return to Fort Stanton, we heard shots and were guided here by this man, *Ernesto*." Fellows continues to address Holton, as he waves a trooper over. "If you are in need of medical attention, I can offer our services at the fort's infirmary."

Holton presses his hand against the bandage under his shirt and glances at the bullet-riddled home of the old woman. "I need to take care of some business here first."

Easing his mount closer to Holton, Ernesto peers down at the man's bleeding wound. "Señor Lang, I will oversee the final care of the old woman. She has no family and has long prepared us for her wishes on this day."

Holton considers the proposal and nods his consent. "Thanks. I don't suppose I'd be of much help in this condition." He looks to Fellows, as the major orders the men to form up. "Major, if it's okay by you, I'll be accompanying you to the fort. A visit to your doctor would be appreciated."

Del Rio Hondo

Major Fellows assesses Holton's injury. "Very well... Are you fit to ride?"

"I can make it."

With a glance to Ernesto, Fellows humorously adds, "Or, at least, he'll die trying."

"Sí, Señor..." Ernesto dismounts and looks at them. "Señor Lang, I will come to see you at the fort after the final arrangements are made for the old woman."

Feeling a bit faint, Holton nods his head and slides his rifle into the saddle scabbard. "I would appreciate knowin' that she was well taken care of."

Fellows notices that Holton is teetering in the saddle and directs his cavalryman to steady him. "Private Simmons... Please escort Mister Lang. He is in need of medical attention."

Holton looks over at the trooper with appreciation. "Private... I might need some help keepin' the horse between me 'nd the ground."

Major Fellows raises an open hand in signal to his troopers. "Very well... If all is in order, we will be on our way. *Hooo...*" With a forward sweep of his hand, the patrol follows in step. Holding his own horse by the headstall, Ernesto steps back to watch the US Cavalry parade out of the village.

~*~

Sitting in the shade of the adobe barn, Jules finishes tying the last leather strips of his braided rope. He looks to Leticia for her approval, and she nods. Standing, he pulls the riata through his hands and competently coils it. His attention is caught by the sound of an approaching horse, and he looks up to see Francisco riding in.

Noticing them gathered at the barn, Francisco rides over. He looks down at the rope in Jules' hand and smiles proudly. "That is a fine braid on the riata you have there, Señor Ward. Come calving season, if you learn how to toss it well, I may have use for you."

Jules looks up at Francisco and starts to make a loop. "I've been practicin'."

Francisco takes up his own rope and laughs heartily. "Sí... But, it may take more than just a few days, or even weeks, to call you a vaquero."

Twirling the loop over his head, Jules appears to know what he's doing. As young William walks around the corner, Jules tosses the rope. The wide loop sails through the air and lands around the boy's shoulders. Startled, William pulls back. "Hey! What's goin' on?"

Jules gives the rope a playful tug, and William's arms are pinned to his sides. Stating his approval, Francisco comments, "That is very good..."

Intending to remove the rope from William, Jules takes a step forward. Suddenly, a loop sweeps under Jules' foot, wraps around his ankle, and tightens. Jules turns to see that the rancher has roped him. The vaquero chuckles with amusement. "Ahh, but I am still *much* better... Someday with much practice, you can make that rope an extension of your own arm."

Jules tries to kick the loop off, but Francisco backs-up his horse a few steps while dallying the rope on the saddle horn. Leticia laughs, as she watches them playfully tug at one another. William is the first to get free. "Hey, when do *I* get to learn to rope?"

Leticia, standing with the smaller riata she just finished making, walks over to the boy. She hands him the coiled rope and pats him fondly on top of the head. "Here you go, Niño. Now you can practice, too."

Jules eventually kicks the rope off of his leg and then recoils his own riata. He sees William looking at Leticia with the admiration of a grateful child. Feeling a familiar pang of loneliness, he observes them, as the boy gives the motherly figure a thankful hug. Francisco brings his horse up alongside Jules and leans down on the saddle horn. "Tomorrow, Jules... Saddle your pony, and we will go gather cows together."

"What about those railroad men?"

"We will not go far..."

Clutching his rope, Jules wipes a tear from his eye and looks up at Francisco. "Yes, sir."

As the vaquero moves his horse off toward the corral, Jules watches Leticia put her arm around young William as they walk to the cabin. Looking very much like a family unit, Jules can't help but feel envious of the intimate bond.

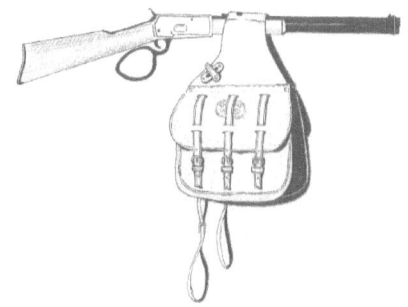

Chapter 17

Holton, laid-up in a military hospital bed with a bandage around his middle, sees the doctor enter the room. Noticing that his patient is awake, the doctor approaches the bedside. "How are you feeling today, Mister Lang?"

"Doin' fine…"

The doctor inspects the bandage. "It is a good thing you came to me when you did. A lot of blood was lost, and infection would have started again if not treated properly."

Holton moves in the bed and tries to stretch out his side. "Thanks for patchin' me up."

"Was it you that dressed the wound earlier?"

"I did a good bit to bugger it up, but it was a woman in the village who cared for the proper healing."

The doctor nods and glances at Holton's blood-stained shirt draped over a chair. "Well, it's a good thing you came in when you did, or things could have turned very serious."

Holton sits up in bed and turns to look out the window. "How long should I lay-up?"

"Few weeks, or for as long as you can stand it, I guess... I've worked on men like you before. Men with bullet holes or arrows sticking out of them... They usually decide to ride to the nearest saloon or brothel before being treated."

Thinking of his friend Bear, he holds back a laugh to keep his side from hurting. "I've known men like that too."

"The best thing to do is let it fully mend, so you don't have to treat it again. It will have to heal, one way or the other, so doing it at the start is recommended."

Holton nods his understanding. "I guess I can hole-up for a few days."

"A month would be preferable."

"We'll see..."

Frowning, the doctor nods and turns away. "Like I said, I've treated folks like you before..." Moving past Dog lying at the foot of the bed, the doctor stops and looks back to Holton. "Oh, and that dog of yours nearly took an orderly's arm off for trying to shoo him outside."

"He comes and goes as he pleases."

"Yes... We noticed. And, Major Fellows allowed for it."

Del Rio Hondo

"We'll be out of here in no time." Dog puts his head down but keeps his eyes on Holton. As the doctor leaves, Holton murmurs to himself. "Not sure what I have to hurry back for, anyway…"

~*~

Riding his Indian pony, Jules works at gathering stray cattle with Francisco. Jules watches, as the vaquero uses his riata to wave the cows along or to occasionally shoot a loop out at one to chase it out of the brush. Noticing a brand on one of the cows, Jules asks, "How do you know which cattle are yours, the neighbors or someone else's?"

"I don't have the neighbors I once did. The railroad has chased most of them off." Jules instinctively glances over his shoulder, reminding himself to be on guard for those men. Easing his mount up alongside Jules, Francisco points to the sideways *G* imprinted on the cow's hip. "That is my own brand, the lazy *G*." He smiles. "You see one of those burned on a skinny bag of bones, you know it is mine." Francisco laughs lightheartedly. "When I moved here years ago, the grass was chest high and green. Plenty of water and grass for everyone… Now, after no good rain for a few years, the grass is dry, and the creeks are low." They both look out to the vast, dry plateau. Francisco comments, "Water is like gold in this hard country. Now that the railroad is here, they want all of it."

"They want your land for the water?"

"Yes, and to create another spur that will reach farther for them and their businesses."

A warm breeze blows past, and Jules feels a flush of indignation swell inside. "They can't just take your land."

They ride along, pushing the three cows ahead of them. "That is what you say. History tells many stories of men taking what is not theirs and calling it progress."

"It's just not right…"

"Sí, mi amigo, but it *is* what it *is*. Life deals you the hand, and you must play it the best you can."

Jules looks at the open stretches of land all around them. "Now that you've chased them off, will they come back again?"

"Yes… I think they will continue to come, until they get what they want."

"Doesn't that worry you?"

Slapping his rope against his thigh, Francisco turns to look at Jules. "Worry about tomorrow takes the joy from today. Let come what may, be it fair or not."

"I could ride to that ranger camp to get help."

To lighten the mood, Francisco grins and gives Jules' leg a smack with his coiled rope. "Let's leave these old cows here, near to the others, and get back. Leticia told me she will make a good dinner and promised us some fresh bread."

The thought of another hearty, homecooked meal with a real family makes Jules smile and feel warm inside. He watches, as Francisco fastens his rope to his saddle and then rides away. After glancing over his shoulder, with the sense that someone is watching, Jules prods his mount and follows.

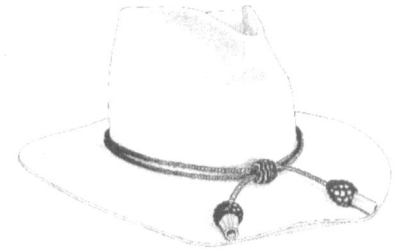

Chapter 18

Inside the railroad district office, Colonel Jackson Henry sits behind a wooden desk. The intricate carvings on its legs and paneled sides match with the other furnishings in the room. Chewing on the stub of a cigar, the colonel looks up at the men standing before him. "What was this man's name?"

Glancing to the posse of men lined up in the room, Sheriff Lowe answers, "Holton Lang."

"Never heard of him… Should I have?"

"Around the time of the war, he was a cavalry scout and dispatch rider. He's bounced around, mostly West Texas since, makin' a name fer himself through several engagements with the natives."

"Mexicans?"

"Mostly Injuns…"

The colonel stares at his desk, then looks up at Lowe and the others. "Where did you finally catch up with him?"

"A spit of a town along the Rio Hondo, jest o'er the border a few days' ride… We hear he has a place in Arizona."

The colonel sits back in his chair and chews on his burnt-out stogie. "Word of this fellow's exploits have put a bit of starch in the spines of the local ranchers. Our job is difficult enough without having some do-good martyr muddying up the waters." He spits a flake of tobacco aside and tosses the cigar away. "I want Holton Lang brought back here to be tried and hung. Let him be an example to those who decide to resist." The sheriff silently looks to the men beside him. Rickter, holding his hat, stands back in the corner. When no one says a word, the colonel adds, "Take care of affairs with Garcia first, and bring me the kid."

Rickter clears his throat. "Which one…?"

The colonel looks from the sheriff to his right-hand man. "Cripes…! How many *are* there?"

"Our men watching the place say there's another younger one that came with the others."

The colonel takes another cigar from a box on his desk and pinches it between his fingers. "Bring in the one who was so full of piss 'n vinegar. The way he talked all uppity to me… He needs a good lesson in the way of manners."

Rickter shrugs. "Someone could get killed."

Del Rio Hondo

Staring stoically at his foreman, Colonel Jackson Henry puts the cigar between his teeth and states, "So be it. Do what you have to do." He takes the stick of tobacco from his mouth, clips the end, and takes a match from the silver tray on his desk. He looks up at the line of waiting men. With no further orders, he strikes the match, waves them off and watches them file out.

~*~

Young William and Alejandra play in the yard, while Leticia prepares food in the shade of the veranda. The boy giggles hysterically, as the girl holds him on the ground, tickling him. The galloping sound of horse hooves alerts them, and they turn to see a dozen riders come up from the arroyo and spread out across the ranchyard. The playful sound of laughter ceases, and the three quietly stand.

Moving his horse nearer, Rickter looks down at them. "Where's Señor Garcia and the other boy?" Leticia starts for the children, but two men on horseback move forward to block her. She waves for the kids to come over, but another rider positions himself to cut them off. Without a word, the woman glares at Rickter and his riders with cold, dark eyes. He flashes a wide grin and snorts. "Not gonna play nice, eh?"

Nudging his horse toward the children, Rickter stares at them with a wicked gleam in his eye. Alejandra tries to embrace William, but a cowboy, as if cutting a calf from its mother, maneuvers his horse between them. Rickter smiles at her, and she avoids his gaze by looking away. So, his attention turns, and he moves his horse closer to the young boy. "Where's yer older brother?"

"He's *not* my brother."

"Well, then… Where's yer *friend*?"

William doesn't respond, so Rickter reaches down and grabs him by the shirt. The stunned boy's feet dangle in the air, as he is easily lifted off the ground. Clenching William's collar, Rickter pulls the boy close to his face and delivers a hard stare into the young man's eyes. "I asked you a question, boy…"

Full of fear, William squirms but can't get free from the foreman's iron grip. Leticia, trying to push past the horseman blocking her, cries, "*Put my boy down!*"

When Rickter turns to look at her, William unexpectedly swings his small fist, striking the foreman square in the nose. As Rickter curses and releases the boy, the horse leaps back. William quickly climbs to his feet and dashes toward Leticia.

Horses snort and skitter about, kicking up dust in the yard as the skilled riders lunge, swerving their mounts to block the three on foot from joining each other. Cut off from Leticia, William moves toward Alejandra, but is violently bumped away by the legs of a blocking horse. Amused with their game, the cowboys herd the three of them like they were livestock, until Rickter fires a shot into the air.

"Gimme that boy, and put the women in the cabin."

Two cowboys reach down, and grab William by a sleeve. The women are pushed together and herded toward the cabin. One of the cowboys holds a calf string and turns his horse to the foreman. "Should we tie 'em?" Another cowboy grabs William's leather riata from where it was hanging on the back of a chair and eagerly holds it up to show the others.

Rickter sees the braided riata and hollers, "Hold it…! Gimme that leather rope. Tie up the women in the soddy and bring the boy to the barn." Two cowboys dismount and take short lengths of rope from their saddle pouches. They take hold of the two protesting women and drag them inside.

Dangling between the cowboys as they ride to the barn, William cries out desperately and struggles to free himself. With a questioning look, the cowboy holding William's leather riata rides to Rickter and hands it over. Flashing a wicked grin, the foreman takes it and makes a wide loop. "I've had enough of all this chasin' around. Garcia and that boy will come to *us*." He swings the loop overhead a few times, tosses the line, and the riata lands around William's neck. Terrified, the young boy continues to squirm, as Rickter leads them all into the barn.

Chapter 19

Jules removes his rope from around the neck of a young calf, after it has been reunited with its mother. He coils the riata and jumps back into the saddle, as Francisco trots from the river. Jules fastens the rope to his saddle and turns to the vaquero. "Did you hear that gunshot?"

As he trots past, Francisco nods his head ominously. "Yes, I did. We should go." Jules spurs his mount to follow.

~*~

Jules and Francisco warily approach the seemingly vacant homestead. They scan the empty yard and look toward the creek for signs of anyone around. All is quiet. Preparing for an ambush, Jules draws his pistol and clicks the hammer back. He whispers over to Francisco. "Where *are* they?"

Jaw clenched, Francisco grimly gazes at each of the buildings. "I will check in the cabin, and you see to the barn." The riders split apart and slowly move to each structure. Francisco dismounts at the cabin door and, with his rifle ready, glances to both sides before stepping in. As Francisco steps into the dark interior, Jules looks to the barn. He rides up and swings the large door open.

Silhouetted by the sunlight streaming in through the doorway, Jules halts his mount at the threshold. He swings a leg over the saddle and steps down. Jules uncocks the hammer on his gun and drops to his knees. Cradling his pistol in his lap, shoulders trembling, he sobs.

Shortly, Francisco appears at the barn doorway with his wife and daughter. At the terrible sight, Leticia lets out a scream and rushes forward to the small pair of boots dangling inches off the ground next to the tail of the braided riata. Wiping tears, Jules climbs to his feet and heads outside to go find his horse. He hears the soft thump of the small body hitting the ground and the wails of the crying women inside. Reaching his horse at the corral fence, Jules opens the saddlebag pouch to find his box of cartridges. He opens it, takes one out, and loads a sixth shell into his handgun.

Coming up from behind, Francisco thoughtfully asks, "What are you going to do?"

Jules holsters his revolver, wipes away a stream of tears and turns to face Fransisco. "I'm gonna kill 'em all!"

"How can you do that?"

Jules pushes the box of ammunition back into his saddlebag and fastens down the flap. "I'll find a way…"

Sensitive to the young man's strong emotions, Francisco tries to dissuade him. "Needlessly throwing your life away will only dishonor the memory of young William."

"I don't care." Jules puts a foot to his stirrup and mounts.

Moving nearer, Francisco pleads, "This is no bueno… Do not go after these men alone."

Staring down at him, Jules clenches his trembling jaw. "What do you *want* me to do?"

In shame, Francisco lowers his gaze and shakes his head. "Please, Hijo… I don't know, but don't go *this* way…

"Come *with* me. They can't be far."

The man looks back to the barn, as the sobbing and wailing continues. He looks at Jules, "Who will care for *them*?"

Looking into the barn, where the women weep over the young boy's body, Jules deeply senses how alone he really is. Tears streaking his face, he looks back to Francisco and utters, "I'll ride to the Texas Ranger camp and get their help."

Francisco puts a gentle hand on Jules' leg and gives it a paternal squeeze. "I am so sorry for what has happened here. Please, come back to us." Choking back his strong emotions, Jules turns his mount, jabs his heels to the pony's flanks and gallops away. He heads eastward, following a fresh trail of horse tracks.

Del Rio Hondo

~*~

Coming over a hill, Jules looks down to a river where three cowboys lounge in the grass while watering their horses. They notice the approach of the lone rider and get to their feet. One of them draws a rifle from a saddle boot as they gather their mounts. Jules keeps his gun hand hanging loose at his side, as he rides up to greet them. "Afternoon, fellas…"

The one with the rifle replies, "Hello, there…"

After looking them over, Jules then gazes to the landscape beyond. "Y'all cowboy for someone nearby?"

Another one answers back. "What's it to you…?"

"I'm lookin' for some fellas who might've rode this way less than an hour ago."

"Ain't seen 'em…"

Jules sees one man bring his horse around, tighten the saddle cinch and mount. When he glances back, the one with the rifle grumbles, "We're jest passin' through."

With a hardened stare, Jules studies the mounted one while keeping a cautious eye on the other two. "You pass through a place jest o'er yonder…?"

As Jules gestures behind, the horseback man impatiently turns to his two companions. "Nope… We ain't bin there."

"Which way you headed?"

"East."

"Mind if I ride with you a spell?"

The mounted cowboy suddenly lunges his horse toward Jules and reaches out to grab him. "Let's *git* 'im, boys…!" Simultaneously, one cowboy on the ground

97

Eric H. Heisner

takes hold of Jules' leg, and the mounted one grabs him by the sleeve. The cowboy with the rifle levers a round into the chamber and points the barrel at Jules.

In the blink of an eye, Jules shakes his arm loose, draws his pistol and shoots the man holding his leg. Thumbing the hammer back, he fires again, killing the cowboy with the rifle. The wounded man alongside Jules stumbles back from the horses, pulls his sidearm and cocks it. Jules spins his mount, knocking the man off-balance, and then fires off another shot. The man pitches to the ground, dead.

The last of the three cowboys quickly assesses the situation and turns his horse to flee. Pivoting in the saddle seat, Jules snaps a shot off, misses and then fires another. With only one shot remaining, Jules holsters his sidearm and kicks his pony into pursuit, leaving the dead cowboys where they lay.

Chapter 20

The nimble Indian pony slowly gains on the rider it's chasing. As Jules nears the fleeing cowboy, he sees that one of his shots must have hit its mark, because traces of blood are splattered on the back of the cantle and on the hindquarters of the horse. Trailing by only a few yards, he kicks his mount harder while unfastening his riata from the saddle. Running at full gallop, Jules swings a loop over his head. He twirls the rope a few times and tosses it forward. The riata's loop sails through the air to land around the man's head and shoulders.

Attempting to free himself, the cowboy pushes the loop up around his neck, just as Jules gives the leather rope a quick jerk to tighten the line. In a fluid motion, Jules dallies the riata around his saddle horn and pulls his mount to a skidding halt. The sudden tension on the rope gives a loud snap and pulls the fleeing cowboy from the saddle. Before he hits the ground, there is a bone-breaking sound of the man's neck cracking.

As the riderless horse continues to trot toward town, Jules unwinds his rope from the saddle horn and dismounts. He walks up, sees that the man is dead and reaches down to loosen the rope. Coiling the riata, he looks up to see a dozen more riders suddenly gathered and almost upon him.

Jules looks to his sweat-soaked pony and realizes that any chase would be short-lived. As the horsemen encircle him, Jules goes for the extra box of ammunition in his saddle pouch. The click of firearms stops him in his tracks.

Rickter, at the forefront of the group, shakes his head. "Kid, I figgered you were a dumbass, but thought ya'd have more sense than to face down *this* many in a fight." With his hand still stuck in his saddlebag, Jules merely glares at him. Rickter waves his men forward. "Grab 'im…"

When one of them rides up, Jules pulls his pistol and fires, dropping the man from the saddle. But, before Jules can retrieve more cartridges from his saddlebag, several other riders descend upon him.

~*~

Ruffed up, and looking worse for wear, Jules is ushered into the railroad headquarters in Big Spring. Shuffling papers at his desk, the colonel studies the young man before him. Smiling, he sits back to scold Jules. "Well, well… You can't say you hadn't been warned." Jules spits blood from his mouth and looks up with his blackened eye and swollen jaw.

The colonel looks to where Jules just spit on his rug and then turns his attention to Rickter. "What of Garcia?"

"He warn't around, but I think he'll git the message."

"I want to be laying track through that plot of land as soon as possible." He turns back to Jules. "How old are you?"

Jules remains silent, so Rickter slaps him upside the head. "Someone asks ya a question, ya answer. Got it, kid?"

When Jules merely turns to glare at Rickter, the colonel waves it off. "No matter. You will be punished for your crimes. The question is... How do we get your friend, Holton Lang, back here to stand trial?"

Jules turns his stare to the colonel. "He won't come."

The gentleman behind the desk rocks back, grinning. "Oh, he will. One way or another..." Swiveling in his chair, he ponders options. "We can't legally hang an underage boy..." He looks to Richter, who shrugs, and then turns back to Jules. "*Publicly*, that is... Yes, Holton Lang will have to do."

Waving the men away, Colonel Jackson Henry looks to the papers on his desk and picks up a pen. "Take the boy out of here and keep him secure. Garcia and his kin need to be gone by the week's end." As the men file out with Jules, the colonel calls after them,

Eric H. Heisner

"Send for Sheriff Lowe, and tell him he will be getting another chance at bringing in Holton Lang."

~*~

Outside the Fort Stanton infirmary, Holton steps to his saddled horse and notices Dog sitting in the shade of the porch. He tilts his head, as he slides his rifle into the saddle sheath. "Hey, Dog... Time for us to go." Lifting a foot to the stirrup, Holton takes a breath and eases himself up. The soreness of his injury causes him to wince, and he looks down at the blood-crusted stain on his buckskin shirt, where the white bandage shows through the hole. Turning his horse, with dog following, he rides away from the activity of the fort.

Beyond the outer boundary of the military grounds, Holton stops his mount, stretches his sore side and looks down at the dog. He snorts a laugh, as he peers back at the outpost. "Ya know, Dog, that was strange..." The dog sits, turns to look back and then looks up, as Holton continues. "This may well've been the first time we've left a military garrison, where we weren't on a job or in some sort of trouble." After staring at the fort, the canine sniffs the air and barks. Holton scans around, touches his heels to his horse and rides on.

Chapter 21

Slumped over in his saddle, Holton travels at a steady pace. Fatigued due to his aching wound, he is feeling his age. Cresting a high plateau, Holton looks around to see Dog scamper out from the bushes ahead. When the canine gives a bark and lifts its nose to sniff the wind, Holton halts his mount. He turns in the saddle and squints to study the trail behind him. After a bit, he turns to look down at his scruffy companion. "Yeah... I see 'im." Dog stands beside panting and lets out a soft whine. Holton considers the lone rider following their trail. "Not much to do about it, other'n wait for him to catch up." Nudging his horse, he continues westward.

~*~

With his horse tied nearby, Holton sets up camp in an abandoned cliff-dwelling. Through a window, he spots the rider that is following him. Keeping to the cover of trees makes it hard to properly identify him. Holton glances over where the watchful canine lies studying the landscape. "Ya think it's one of them railroad men? Or, someone from the sheriff's posse...?" Dog turns his head toward Holton and lets his tongue hang out while breathing in panting breaths. Holton grimaces and looks back to where the rider last was. He shakes his head. "I'm too tired to play this game." With a whine, Dog closes his mouth and puts his chin to his front paws. Holton turns back to Dog. "Yeah...? Well, you're not gettin' any younger, either."

~*~

A small campfire lights up the rock-stacked walls of the cliff dwelling. His makeshift bed laid out, Holton reclines with his rifle at his side. At the sound of hooves on the rocky terrain, Dog lets out a whimper. Holton glances over and whispers, "Yeah... I hear 'im."

As the rider gets nearer, Holton moves his rifle across his lap and levers the action with a loud clicking sound. Suddenly, the clopping of hooves stops, and a familiar voice calls out from the darkness. "Hallo, the camp..."

Instantly recognizing the man's heavy accent, Holton uncocks his rifle. "Ernesto...?"

The rider comes closer, dismounts, and steps into the firelight. "Sí, Señor Lang... You are a hard man to follow."

Amused, Holton looks aside to Dog and then down at his wound. "Not really..."

Holding his horse's reins, Ernesto approaches the camp. An exuberant smile lights up his dark features, and he laughs. "Well, I am not a good tracker, and I have a very slow horse."

From the other side of the campfire, Holton inquires, "Are you alone?"

"No... I am here with *you*."

Holton grimaces. "Did you *follow* me *by yourself?*"

"Sí... The farming life in that tiny village is not for me. After we bury the star-gazing woman, there is nothing interesting left for me there."

"What about your family?"

Ernesto shrugs. "All work and no play is how they live. You know what you get for that?"

"No."

"You get dead like everyone and nothing to show for it."

Holton is intrigued. Nodding in agreement, he asks, "What'll you get following me?"

Ernesto ties his horse to a rock and sits by the fire. "Better scenery than the hind-end of a plow animal."

"Where do you think I'm goin'?"

Ernesto shrugs. "I don't know."

"I was headed back to my ranch in Arizona."

"You work a ranch?"

This time, Holton shrugs, watching as Ernesto eyes jerky laid out on the saddlebag. "Not much..."

The Mexican smiles. "You are *my* kind of rancher."

"You hungry...?"

Del Rio Hondo

"Sí, mucho... I ate my food on the first day." Holton tosses him the jerky and Ernesto takes a bite.

"Why would you do that?"

Ernesto chews awhile and then looks up to the night sky. "I didn't know how far you were going."

"It's a fair bit..."

"I have never ventured into the wilderness far or gone more than a day from my village."

Holton looks at the dark landscape and then back to Ernesto. "What'd you do for food if *I* wasn't here?"

Ernesto thinks, glances at Dog and the canine groans. The Mexican flashes a grin and points a piece of jerky at Dog. "He looks mangy, but would be very tasty."

Seeing how Dog warily eyes Ernesto, Holton can't help but laugh. "You'd have to catch him first."

Feeling much better with a bit of food in his stomach, Ernesto grins wider. "I think I could... He limps, sometimes. And, I could get him while he naps." Chin down on his paws, Dog glances over to Holton and then back at the Mexican man. He lets out a low, rumbling growl. Ernesto rubs his hands together hungrily. "Mmm...Very tasty indeed."

Holton laughs and tosses Ernesto another strip of jerky. "Here... Eat this, instead."

"Muchas gracias."

Laying back against his gear, Holton sets his rifle aside. "So, you plan to ride along with me, then?"

"Sí, if you'll have me..."

"Do I have a choice in the matter?"

Ernesto smiles, as he chews. "No, Señor."

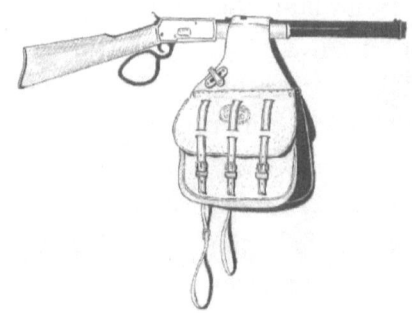

Chapter 22

In the morning, curled up under his horse blanket, Ernesto lies sleeping next to the ashes of the campfire. Holton, rifle in hand, steps to the edge of the cliff and looks out over the valley. Steadily, his eyes scan the horizon, until they pause to focus on a far-off cloud of rising dust.

Ernesto stirs behind him. "What is it?"

"Riders…"

"How many?"

"More'n a few…"

Ernesto climbs out from under his blanket and goes over to squat near Holton. Gazing out, he asks, "Are they after you?"

Del Rio Hondo

Surprised, Holton looks sideways at the sleepy Mexican. "Why would you think that?"

Ernesto shrugs. "You seem to be very popular."

Looking back out to the distant, rising cloud of dust, Holton ponders possible numbers, purpose, and destination. "Travelin' west… Could be homesteaders or a cavalry patrol."

"Or Indians?"

"That's possible…"

Ernesto mutters, "Or, could be a sheriff's posse."

"I think we're rid of them by now."

"*Maybe…*"

Wondering if he might know more than he's saying, Holton glances at Ernesto and then goes to sit by his saddle. "Whoever it is, they're not following too close on our trail, and we'll let them pass before movin' on."

Ernesto returns to his gear and sits on his blanket. "What's for breakfast?"

"Whatever you hunt up."

Ernesto gives a humorous glance toward Dog, who looks back at him and growls. "Maybe I can hunt us a wild pig to eat or possibly a fat turkey?"

Carefully reclining against the seat of his saddle, Holton winces in pain. "Whatever you find, try not to shoot the hell out of it and attract any attention."

Like a dangerous man, the Mexican draws his stag-handled belt knife and waves it around. "I have killed many a bird with just my blade." Seeking Holton's approval, Ernesto adds some clarification. "Only, they were in my uncle's yard."

Holton sets his hat aside. "Yeah? Wild turkeys...?"

"No, not really... They were raised there and knew no other home, but they did give a good chase."

With a grimace, Holton lays his head back. "I'm gonna git more rest. Take Dog, and he'll flush something out."

"You sleep, my friend. I will find us something to eat." Ernesto stands and tucks his knife away. "C'mon, Dog...!" After sitting up and noticing that Holton is preparing to sleep, Dog stares at Ernesto for a moment and scampers off.

~*~

Inside the cliff-dwelling, a small fire crackles as it cooks a long, stringy jackrabbit hanging from a makeshift spit. Ernesto turns the stretched carcass over to roast the other half. From the other side of the campfire, Holton watches while reminiscing on days back at the ranch. Ernesto smiles at him. "What is that look, Señor?"

"Just thinking on that rabbit..."

"You like them very much?"

Holton lets out a laugh. "I know *someone* who does..."

Ernesto glances to where Dog is chewing on several pieces of uncooked carcass. "That dog of yours is not much on sharing. He got two rabbits for him, and I only got one for us."

"He's independent..."

"Y con mucha hambre." Holton watches the glistening fat from the skinned rabbit drip into the fire and flare up. Ernesto evens it out by turning the spit. He looks to Holton. "When we get to your ranch, I will cook us many good meals." Holton nods. With thoughts of Alice, the woman he left behind, he watches *this* cook take the roasted rabbit off the spit and divide it in half. "You prefer heads or tails?"

"Tail is fine."

Ernesto hands over the hindquarter half and waits for Holton to start eating. He smiles proudly. "Es very good, no?" Holton nods, and Ernesto continues. "I am a *good* cook."

"I'm not a bad cook, myself."

The Mexican grins wider. "Sí, but it *always* tastes better when someone *else* does it."

As the two quietly eat, Dog sits in the corner crunching on small bones. When Holton looks over, Dog looks up, seeming to smile as he licks his chops. After a prolonged silence, Ernesto wipes his mouth and speaks. "How far is it to Arizona and this ranch of yours?"

"A few days yet..."

Ernesto sucks the last of the meat from the tiny bones. "This life in the wild is okay, but I prefer having a nice bed."

Holton chews the meat off, then tosses his finished bones into the fire. "How are you at building houses?"

From across the campfire, the Mexican smiles and nods. "Excelente... I am a fine builder of adobe and stacked rock."

"We can keep you plenty busy, then."

Ernesto glances to the canine and looks back at Holton. "Who is *we*? You and the dog?"

"There might be some folks around at my place yet when we get there."

"Your family?"

"Sort of…"

Ernesto peels off some crispy skin from the rabbit's head and eats it. "I look forward to meeting your people, Señor Lang. Thank you for bringing me along."

"I didn't *bring* you… You just *came*."

Ernesto smiles and nods. "Then thank you for *letting* me come along on your journey." The two sit by the fire finishing their meal, as the evening sky begins to darken and faint stars appear in the sky.

Chapter 23

Holton and Ernesto continue westward, with Dog scampering through the brush ahead of them. Moving into higher country, the trees change from scrubby desert plants to large pines. Inhaling the crisp, fresh air, the Mexican peers all around. "Ahhh, this place reminds me of home."

Holton glances over. "Homesick already…?"

"No, it only reminds me of when I was a young boy and the feeling of freedom."

Touching his wound, as he thinks back to living with a native tribe in his younger days, Holton nods in agreement. "Nothing is freer than a boy runnin' wild."

Curious, Ernesto turns to Holton. "You grow up wild?"

"Yep… With the Apache…"

Ernesto's eyes go wide. "You live with *Apache?*"

Holton adjusts himself in the saddle and looks over at his shocked companion. "My mother was one…"

The two travel silently for a while, until Ernesto speaks. "How you come to be like you are?"

"My father dealt trade goods. We traveled around and, when he was gone, I stayed at the fort."

"You live with Apache and then live at a fort?"

"I was near grown, so they kept me on to do odd jobs."

Ernesto dwells on Holton's rare experience growing up. At length, he offers, "My life was boring until I meet *you.*"

Holton shrugs. "It's just life…"

"Yes, but you seem to live more of it than others."

~*~

Traveling the road up to the ranch, Holton and Ernesto spot a trickle of smoke coming from the chimney of the cabin. Not able to see the entire cabin, Ernesto hungrily sniffs the air. "It smells like your old friends know you're coming and are preparing us a *welcome home* dinner."

As they ride through the ranch gate, Holton keeps his gaze focused on the horizon. Ernesto notices the JN5 brand on the crossbar. "Is that your cattle brand?"

"That's the brand of my ol' friend, Charlie Nichols, who was the previous owner."

"He is gone somewhere?"

"Dead..."

"I'm sorry."

"No need to be... Happens to everyone."

Entering the yard, Holton notices that, over by the barn, behind an unhitched wagon, there are more than a few horses in the corral. Scanning the area, he spies the unfinished house that he and Bear were working on months ago. Moving up to the initial cabin's front porch, they can smell the cookfire. Twisting in the saddle, Ernesto looks around for any people and then mutters out loud. "I wonder what's cooking?"

In the shade of the porch, the door of the cabin opens, and Holton is more than surprised to see Jules step outside. "What are you doing *here* boy?"

Bear and a very pregnant Alice step out behind Jules. Bear anxiously scratches his scruffy beard. "Hello there, Holton, you ol' Johnny-come-lately..."

A cold chill runs up Holton's spine, as several men with rifles file out and onto the porch. Lastly, Sheriff Lowe steps out, grins at Holton and hooks a thumb on the top of his gunbelt. "Well, if'n it ain't Holton Lang..."

Ernesto gulps, and then looks over to Holton. "Unexpected visitors?" Holton glances at Ernesto and then down to his rifle in the saddle scabbard.

Sheriff Lowe calls out. "Don't grab for that gun, or who knows who could get killed."

Keeping both hands stationary, Holton studies Jules' swollen jaw and blackened eye, and then he glances to Bear, who looks as rough as ever. "You okay, Bear?"

"Fine, I guess... These friends of yourn?"

"Not hardly..." His gaze travels to Alice's round midsection and then quickly back to Bear. "She *pregnant...?* What *happened?*"

Bear merely shrugs. "You bin gone a long time..."

The sheriff steps forward, pushes Bear aside and raises his rifle. He stops at the top step of the porch and orders, "Unbuckle yer gunbelt and step down from those horses..." When his gaze darts to Ernesto, he regards the Mexican's shaggy mount with curiousity. "The both of ya..."

Del Rio Hondo

Holton unbuckles his belt and holster, lets them drop, and then dismounts. "Why are you here?"

Rifle held ready, Sheriff Lowe stares directly at Holton. "Yer goin' back to Texas with us."

"Why back to Texas?"

"There's a noose waitin' fer ya."

Holton looks to Jules, to Bear, and then to Alice. Then, he looks back at the sheriff and asks, "You came just for me...?"

Stomping down the porch steps, the sheriff considers the blood-crusted wound on Holton's shirt. He steps right up to face Holton. "Don't you worry, Lang. You'll have company." He waves for two of the gunmen on the porch to move down and join them. When the sheriff subtly nods to one of them, the man takes his rifle butt and slams it against the back of Holton's head, knocking him out cold.

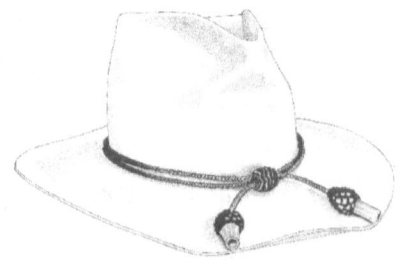

Chapter 24

Inside the ranch barn, Holton wakes up slumped against the side of a stall. Beside him are Jules and Ernesto. Hands tied, seated across from them, Bear and Alice lean back on the wood-slat outer wall. Wincing at the throbbing pain in his head, Holton slowly blinks his eyes and looks to his friend, Bear. "What's been going on here?"

Disgruntled, Bear huffs a breath and grumbles back. "We thought *you* might have some answers for *us*."

Holton's gaze turns to Alice and then down to her swollen belly. Clenching his teeth, he angrily looks back at Bear. "What'd you *do?*"

In return, the old scout's eyes go wide. He sputters, "Don't ya look at *me* like that!"

Holton replies, "I ain't been gone *that* long."

Del Rio Hondo

"Long 'nough...!"

"*Thanks a lot*, pard. *For taking care* of things..."

Alice sees Holton's jealousy and realizes his mistake. "Hold it, you two!" They all look at her, as she gestures to Bear. "You think this is *his* baby?!?"

With Holton glaring at him, Bear shakes his head and guffaws. "No, siirrreeee! That's *yer* doin'!!!"

Still not quite relieved, Holton turns again to Alice. "Why didn't you *tell* me?"

Completely shocked, she stares back at him. "*When?* You've been gone for *months*!"

Holton is taken aback. "I just... Just... I didn't know." He sighs and glances back to Bear.

Smoothing her hand over her rounded midsection, Alice calms herself. "I had no idea until after you left, and then there was no tellin' when you would be back."

With a grunt, Bear adds, "Or, who ya'd be bringin' with ya when ya *did* show up again... Jest who *are* these guys?"

Holton turns to Jules and takes a better look at his injuries. "How ya doin' kid? Things not go as planned...?"

Having been silent thus far, Jules looks up. "I'm sorry, Holton. You warned me to stay out of it."

Holton give a nod. "There's nothin' to be sorry about. I've been in trouble before."

Bear snorts. "He kinder attracts it..."

After shooting Bear a scolding glance, Holton turns back to Jules. "What happened with that family?"

Eric H. Heisner

The young man looks at Alice and Bear, and then back to Holton with his eyes glazed over with tears. "Those railroad men killed young William."

As Alice instinctively touches her belly, Bear mutters, "Who's William...?"

Sympathetic, Holton lowers his gaze and bows his head. "He was a good kid... And, he had a little more time in this life because of you."

"I got him killed."

"Things happen in life that you have no control over."

As more tears drop, Jules looks down to his lap. "If I would've kept out of it, like you said, he would still be alive..." He looks over at the bloodstain on Holton's buckskin shirt. "You wouldn't have gotten shot, these men wouldn't be here, and we wouldn't be in this trouble."

They are silent, until Holton speaks again. "Life is gonna play out the way it wants, no matter what you do to try and steer it. Tomorrow isn't guaranteed for anyone... So, you hav'ta make the best of what you're given today."

Jules murmurs, "William doesn't *have* a tomorrow."

Breaking the somber mood, Ernesto pipes in. "Oh, well. We may not, either."

When everyone looks at the Mexican, Alice inquires, "And, *who* are *you*?"

"I am a good friend of Señor Lang."

Del Rio Hondo

Holton nods in reply. "Back at Rio Hondo, he helped me out of a tight spot with that sheriff you just met."

Bear looks from Ernesto to Holton. "Rio Hondo? Where's that?"

"Near Fort Stanton..."

Bear nods, reminiscing on his former military career at the many different forts. "You always do attract a followin'..." Bear looks around and lifts his nose to sniff. "Speakin' of that, where's that smelly dog of yourn?"

Slightly irritated, Holton realizes that Dog didn't offer them any warning when they rode up to the ranch, and that he hasn't seen him since. He tilts his head to look outside the barn, scans the limited view and is disappointed. "Ain't seen him since we got here. Probably wouldn't have made much of a difference anyway..."

Twisting his hands against the rope bindings, Bear looks at Holton. "These fellas arrived jest a few days 'fore you. Seemed sure you were due back and were intent on meetin'... What d'ya s'pose they plan on doin' now?"

Overhearing the last portion of their conversation, Sheriff Lowe steps into the barn and offers, "We intend to take Mister Lang back to Texas and *hang* 'im."

Alice holds her round belly, silently fighting back her emotions, while Bear cranes his neck to look at the lawman. "Back to Texas...? On who's authority?"

"Mine. As a sheriff."

121

"If ya haven't noticed, ya ain't in Texas no more."

The sheriff grins. "That's why we don't jest hang 'im here 'n be done with it."

Jules tries to dry his eyes and then looks up at the sheriff. "They intend to chase off all the homesteaders in the path of the railroad and don't care who they have to lynch to do it. Innocent children be damned..."

Holton looks over at Jules and then back at the sheriff. "You killed that boy?"

"That wasn't *my* doin'..."

Jules snarls, "Yer a part of it!"

The sheriff shifts his attention from Jules to address all the captives. "I have a warrant for Mister Lang. He gunned down several innocent folks and has to answer for it."

Righteously, Holton replies, "I didn't shoot *anyone* who didn't come at *me* first."

Bear grumbles, "Sounds 'bout right..."

The sheriff moves further into the barn. "Doesn't matter. You and the kid are comin' back to Texas."

Holton looks across to his old friend and the pregnant woman sitting beside him. "What about *them?*"

Sheriff Lowe looks at Bear and Alice, and then curiously to Ernesto. "I don't know where you picked up the Mexican, but we have no use for an old man and his pregnant wife." Silent, in protest, Bear clenches his jaw, as Alice rolls her eyes at the notion of them being a romantic couple.

Ernesto sits up. "I go where Señor Lang goes."

The sheriff glances at him and shrugs nonchalantly. "Then, we'll hang you, too."

Del Rio Hondo

Deflated, Ernesto mumbles, "Or, I *could* stay *here*."

The sheriff waves some of his men into the barn, and Holton looks them over. "When do we leave?"

"No time like the present…" He ushers them forward, and the men tug Holton and Jules to their feet. Jules looks from Holton to Bear, who nods sympathetically, as the boy is shoved toward the door.

Holton's gaze connects with Alice, and he meekly offers, "Sorry I can't stay longer."

She replies, "It's always something…"

Holton is escorted out of the barn after Jules, and the sheriff stands over the remaining three. "The question now is what to do with the rest of you…" They look up at the sheriff, waiting for their sentence. "If we cut ya free, you'd prob'ly follow 'n muck up the works, so we'd have to kill ya anyway."

Bear grunts, "Ya gonna do away with us now, instead?"

Sheriff Lowe's gaze lingers on the pregnant woman. "Women or children. I ain't keen on murderin' innocent folks."

Bear retorts, "That ain't the impression we get."

The sheriff looks outside to where Holton and Jules are being put on horses and thinks a moment before looking back to the three prisoners. "I'm leavin' two men here to make sure ya stay out of trouble. Their orders will be to wait a few days and then cut ya loose."

Bear looks at the attractive woman next to him and then back at the sheriff. "You *trust* these men…?"

The sheriff shakes his head. "Not at all, but that's what's got to be done." He turns on his heel, waving as he departs. "Good luck to you all."

Sitting up straighter, Ernesto looks across to Bear and then to Alice. "What will we do?"

Alice tugs at the ties around her wrists. "We're not going to sit here and wait for them to kill us."

Chapter 25

The sheriff's posse of horsemen move steadily eastward, with Holton and Jules mounted between them. His bound hands resting on the saddle horn, Jules turns to quietly whisper, "Holton, I'm sorry…"

"No need… This ain't yer doin'."

"I feel responsible."

"We all make choices and have to deal with the results."

A rider comes up alongside and smacks his rifle barrel into Holton's ribs. "Keep quiet, or I'll be glad to put another bullet in ya fer what ya did to my pals."

Eric H. Heisner

Wincing in pain as he bends to catch his breath, Holton mutters under his breath. "*You* may have one comin' yet..." The rider laughs mockingly but drops back when he gets a scolding look from the sheriff.

After glancing around, Jules whispers again to Holton. "They'll kill us, for sure..."

"Just as soon as we're in Texas."

~*~

At the Nichols ranch, the two the posse left behind share a jug of whiskey, as they lounge on the front porch of the cabin. The smaller of the pair, Clark, looks over at the barn and sighs. "I don't mind knockin' off that crusty ol' man when it's time, but it's a shame to kill a good-lookin' woman."

The burly one, Big Matt, takes the ceramic jug, twists his arm to lift it over his shoulder and takes a swallow. As the strong liquor burns his insides, he looks over to his partner. "What about the Mexican?"

"Yeah? What about 'im?"

"Ya mind killin' *him*...?"

Clark giggles drunkenly. "Nope... I thought ya were gonna say he was good-lookin'!"

Big Matt scratches his tangle of whiskers and mutters, "He *is* kinda purty... Not fat, like that woman."

Wondering if he's joking or not, Clark stares at Matt and then takes the jug. "She's got a *baby* in there, ya dufus."

Matt looks confused. "How d'ya know...?"

"That's the kinda fat they git..."

Del Rio Hondo

His thoughts muddled by alcohol, Big Matt thinks before responding, "But, when we *got* here, it was jest that old man and her…"

Clark nods assuredly. "Yep… I know 'bout such things. Sometimes women get horned-up, too, and they'll take whatever's around when they *need* it."

"Even if ya don't *pay* 'em?"

"Sure… Jest look at that ol' codger in there…"

For a moment, they contemplate the concept in silence. The big one is the first to speak up. "I still prefer the Mex…"

"You can *have* 'im."

Big Matt is satisfied. "We still have to kill 'em all?"

"Yep."

"*Tomorrow…?*"

Clark leans his head back on the rocking chair and starts to nod off. "Tomorrow…"

~*~

Camped alongside a creek, Holton and Jules sit next to each other near the picketed horses. With their hands tied in front, they stare quietly as the sheriff's posse shares a meal. Jules' stomach growls. "Think they'll feed us?"

"I wouldn't bet on it."

"My dang stomach is so empty, it feels like it's scrapin' 'gainst my backbone."

Trying not to think of the food, Holton shifts his uncomfortable position. "It'll be a few days yet."

"Even the Comanche fed us…"

"These men aren't ones to know how to ride a long trail. They ate their fixin's up before and will again on the way back. Keep a clear mind and drink whatever water is offered."

Jules twists his midsection in an attempt to quiet his gut. "Hard to keep a clear mind, when I'm so durned hungry."

With some effort, Holton manages to pull a few dry leaves from a sprig of nearby grass and pass them to Jules. "Chew on this awhile."

"What is it?"

"Grass…"

Jules chews on the thin leaves, grimaces, and swallows. He looks over to Holton and mutters, "Still hungry…"

Smiling, Holton imparts a bit of wisdom. "Remember… It's just a feeling, like any other."

Trying to distract his thoughts from the smell of food, Jules surveys the landscape, looking for any hope of rescue. "You seen Dog lately?"

"Nope…"

Jules peers around, listening closely for movement in the nearby brush. "I can't tell if he's near or not."

"We all got to be somewhere."

Chapter 26

The three prisoners inside the barn are bound and asleep. Alice lies down with her head nestled on Bear's lap, while he sits uncomfortably with his tied hands pinned behind his back. The door creaks and Bear opens an eye. Early morning light spills in through the opening and soft footsteps approach.

Leaning over for a better look, Bear breathes a sigh of relief when he sees the dark eyes of Dog staring back at him. "You do show up at the darnedest times…"

The dog gives the barn's interior a probing sniff and then looks to where Ernesto sleeps on the opposite side of the stall. Bear looks again to the doorway and then back at the canine. "Did ya bring a knife blade maybe, or something useful?"

Looking at Bear innocently, Dog sits on his haunches and lets his tongue roll out to pant. Bear stares at him a while, then grunts, "Huh..."

~*~

Holton and Jules ride encircled by the sheriff's posse. Holton glances around and then secretly whispers over to Jules. "I saw something back there in the brush. Keep ready..."

"Dog...?"

"I don't think so."

Jules looks back and sees only the men on horseback. "Could be Bear has come to rescue us?"

Holton smiles. "Doubt it. He was never very stealthy."

"Injuns...?"

"Could be... Just stay at the ready."

The group continues the trek back to Texas, as the call of a lone coyote echoes off the distant rocks.

~*~

Daylight streams in through the barn's open doorway. Hungover, the two posse members shuffle in and head down the center aisle. They stop at the last stall and consider the three restrained prisoners. The smaller one, Clark, coughs and spits. "Time to git up 'n go."

As Bear rouses, he sees the heavyset man go over and give Ernesto a kick. The Mexican, hands tied behind him, wakes with a start and sits up straight. "*Que pasa...?*"

Bear grunts, "They come to kill us now."

Alice opens her eyes. She touches her belly and groans. "What's going on?"

Del Rio Hondo

Walking past Bear, Clark stumbles on a piece of wood. He looks down and grabs at an oak handle to reveal its axe buried in the straw. His suspicious gaze darts to Bear. "*Wow...!* Must'a missed *this* before..." Noticing that the old man's hands are securely tucked behind his back, Clark smiles with relief. "Guess *you* did, too... Else, we'd a'had trouble, most likely."

Bear's kicks with his boot and catches Clark in the shin, sending the man reeling in pain. "You *still* got trouble, pal!" Bear begins to rise and is quickly put down by a smashing blow from Big Matt. Bear's head bangs back against the wall of the stall and, dazed, he slumps down.

Balling his fist for another blow, the big man thunders, "Sit yer ass down!" Holding his hurt leg, Clark limps over to glare at Bear. He raises the axe head, and Matt stops him. "You'll make a mess of the woman, if ya hit her accidental..."

Clark lowers the sharp blade and ogles Alice. He tosses the axe aside and pulls her up by the arm. "C'mon, woman... Yer gonna make me some breakfast."

Big Matt heaves a chuckle and turns to grab Ernesto from the floor, "And *you's* gonna be *dessert!*" Fear fills the Mexican's eyes, as the huge man roughly pulls him to his feet. Ernesto stares at Bear in disbelief, while he is dragged through the barn after Clark and Alice.

As the men drag the prisoners from the barn, a low, rumbling growl stops them in their tracks. They are surprised to see a dog before them, teeth bared and ready to attack. Taking a step back, the smaller man declares, "*What the hell...?*"

Curious, Big Matt tilts his head as he looks toward Dog. "I think I've seen that ugly dog before..."

Positioning Alice in front to block him from an attack, Clark turns to his partner. "*Where...?*"

"That Mex village we got run off from."

"It followed us all the way *here*?"

Dog growls again and advances slowly. In unison, both men take a step back. Big Matt proclaims, "Hell, I don't think that feller has *two* of them ugly dogs..."

Keeping his eyes on the snarling canine, Clark whispers, "Go git that axe..."

Big Matt shakes his head. "*You* git it..."

"Dammit! Let go that Mex, and *git* the damn *axe!*"

Begrudgingly, he releases Ernesto and creeps backward to the barn. As he turns around and steps through the doorway, a solid whack is followed by a faint whimper.

Clark momentarily takes his attention off the dog to look back into the barn. Pivoting around and stepping from inside, Big Matt painfully looks down at the axe handle protruding from his burly torso, the blade buried deep beneath his ribs. Clark gasps, "What the hell...?!?"

At that moment, in a flash of sharp teeth and claws, Dog charges to attack Clark. Tumbling back under the snarling canine, the man releases his hold on Alice.

His hands free, Bear steps out of the barn and lands a fist to Big Matt's jaw. The man with the axe in his belly falls to the ground and twists up into a pained ball. Bear reaches down, grabs the handle of the axe, and his gaze is met by the man's horrified expression. "Nooo…!"

Bear yanks out the blade and blood gushes from the gaping wound. He gives Big Matt a kick to the head and renders him nearly unconscious. Turning to the ravaging canine attack on Clark, Bear walks over with the bloody axe. "That's enough, Dog."

Dog releases his snarling grip and takes a step back. Breathing heavily, cradling ragged bite-wounds, Clark peers over toward his laid-out partner. Then, he looks up to see Bear holding the bloody weapon. "Wha… What're ya gonna do?" Bear glances over to where Alice sits in the dirt with her bound hands clutching her pregnant belly. Clark whimpers, "Hold it, we weren't gonna *hurt* her…"

Adjusting his grip on the blood-smeared handle, Bear takes a deep, calming breath. He stares at the chewed-up man snivelling before him and then briefly looks back to Alice. Climbing to her feet, she brushes off her dress and announces, "Bear, if *you* don't do it, I *will*."

Wide-eyed, Clark raises his hands up to cover his head, as Bear heaves the bloody axe. "*Wait…!*" With a heavy thud, the blade swings down, and several finger pieces fly to the side. There is a soft whimper from the dying man, and Bear releases the slippery handle, leaving the blade deep in the man's skull.

When Bear looks back to Alice, she asks, "When did you get your hands free?"

Bear turns to Dog, now sitting calmly next to Ernesto. "Hate to say it, but that is one useful dog…"

Alice walks over to the big man on the ground with the gaping belly wound and draws his knife from its sheath. Looking up at her, the man groans faintly. With her hands still tied in front, she grips the knife, and plunges it deep into the man's neck. Straightening up, she looks at Bear and remarks, "Like butchering a hog." Bear stands, speechless, as Alice offers him the bloody knife. "Don't just stand there looking stupid… *Cut me free.*"

Flashing a grin, Bear jumps to it. "*Yes, ma'am!*"

Chapter 27

As the sheriff's posse travels eastward, they notice some ancient cliff dwellings in the distance. One of the men points to the primitive village, and he suddenly lets out a wail when an arrow pierces his hat and buries itself in his head. The riders around him stare in astonishment as the shaft protrudes from the man's hat without killing him.

Sheriff Lowe whirls his horse around and calls out to them. "Stop *starin'* at 'im, *dammit! And git to cover!*"

Jules looks to Holton. "Now?"

"Yes, *now!*"

They kick their mounts. But, before they can bolt away, other riders grab their horses by the headstalls

Del Rio Hondo

and hold them back. Sheriff Lowe draws his pistol and aims it at Holton, declaring, "Come with us, or I can kill ya now."

With bound hands, Holton points to the ruins. "Head for those cliff dwellings! We can hold out there."

The sheriff fires his pistol toward movement in the brush and then waves his hand to the north. "Head to those rocks. Keep close and follow me, boys…"

Another man takes an arrow and falls from the saddle, while the rest of the group wheel their horses around and head for the cliff dwellings. The posse hastily retreats with several horseback natives in pursuit. Riding beside Holton and Jules, another posse member tumbles from his horse, while several men aimlessly fire their guns back over their shoulders. Swinging his galloping horse over to them, Sheriff Lowe screams, "Hold yer fire, men, and head fer those ruins!"

The horses slow their pace as they ascend the embankment, climbing the cliff until they can't go any farther. Some of the men dismount to try pulling their horses along. Eventually, the whole posse abandons their horses and scampers up the steep, rocky ridge. Holton and Jules, still bound, also dismount and follow.

Of the original twelve-man posse, only six remain, including the man with the arrow protruding from his hat. Climbing through the scrub brush and boulders, the men gain access to the dwellings under the cliff's edge and shoot downward toward their native attackers. Sticking together, Holton and Jules scoot to the back of the shelter, as the posse defends its position from behind the stacked rock walls. Holding Holton's special rifle, Sheriff Lowe looks back at them. "If I give ya a gun, will ya help to protect this position?"

Eager to help, Jules scoots forward, but Holton reaches out to hold him back. "Is this *yer* fight…?"

Turning to him, the young man asks, *"Isn't it…?"* Holton simply replies with a look.

The sheriff draws his belt knife and tosses it to them. "Cut yerselves loose 'n git *at* it!"

The defending rifles steadily return fire, as arrows lob in the air and bounce off the rock walls and the cliffs. Jules looks to where the knife landed and then back to Holton. Glancing at a feathered shaft laying nearby, Holton mutters, "Likely Apache, and they ain't after us."

A man catches an arrow in the chest, falls back, then crumples and dies at their feet. Jules looks toward the knife again. "They'll kill us all, won't they?"

"Down there possibly, but not in this place…"

Confused, Jules looks to the experienced Westerner. "Ain't these *Indian* homes we're in?"

While using his boot heel to scoot the knife closer to them, Holton shakes his head. "They were built long before the Apache were here. They have stories of who built them, but they won't enter for fear of spirits."

Jules looks to the men shooting down the hillside at targets barely visible. "Do *they* know that?"

Holton shrugs. "Guess not…"

The sheriff looks back at them and sees that their hands are still tied. "You two gonna help or not?"

Holton shakes his head. "Not our fight."

Del Rio Hondo

As he reloads the rifle, Sheriff Lowe looks at Holton incredulously. "It *will* be, when they git up here and cut yer *guts* out 'n let ya watch the wild dogs *eat* at 'em!" He levers the action of the rifle, aims it, and fires toward the attackers below. Beside the sheriff, another man gets hit with an arrow and slumps onto the wall.

Witnessing the desperate fight, Jules whispers to Holton. "I don't *always* have to git in the mix…"

Holton nods and reaches to pick up the sheriff's blade. He cuts his hands free and then slices the young man's ties. "Choose your battles, or they'll choose you." Getting to his feet, Holton crouches down low and scoots up behind the sheriff. The lawman looks at him, holds his shot and draws his pistol. "'Bout damn time…"

Before the sentence finishes, Holton smashes his fist into the sheriff's jaw. As the sheriff falls, Holton snatches the rifle and pistol away and points them at the posse member nearest to him. "Jules. Git that man's gun."

Jules rushes forward to grab the man's rifle and holstered sidearm. Holton pushes the posse member over toward the sheriff and puts a finger to his mouth to shush him. With their guns held on both men, Holton and Jules scoot to the back of the dwelling and wait for the others to notice that some of them aren't fighting anymore.

One by one, the defenders turn to see that their former prisoners are now pointing guns at them. With a cordial smile, Holton motions for them to discard their weapons and move over to join the sheriff.

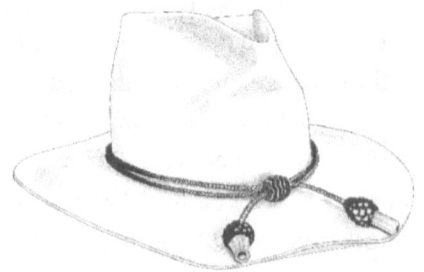

Chapter 28

Both sides have ceased fire. No arrows bounce into the ruins, and the sheriff and his men huddle near the crumbled entrance. The sound of horses catches their attention, and they peer out to see their animals being herded away. Sheriff Lowe turns to Holton. "They're stealin' our horses."

"Are they worth more than your life?"

The sheriff scowls. "They'll come fer *us* next..."

"Maybe..."

"Why don't ya think so?"

Holton's gaze drifts around the room. "The spirits of the ancient people reside in these cliff homes. They would rather take our horses than come in here after us."

Del Rio Hondo

The sheriff looks at his sorry lot of survivors. They all have arrow wounds. He looks to the man with the feathered shaft protruding from his hat. *"Pull that arrow out already!"*

The man is in pain but, apparently not mortally wounded. "I *tried* to jerk it free, and it *won't unstick.*"

Eying the offending arrow, the man beside him grunts, "We *all* tried, and it won't come out."

The shaft wags ridiculously, as the wounded man nods. "I cain't even take my durned *hat* off!"

Flustered, the sheriff shakes his head and looks to another one of his injured men. "What about *him*?"

They all look to see that the quiet soul has passed. Respectfully, one of the men bows his head after lowering the man's eyelids. *"He* don't care no more. He's *dead…"*

The surviving three members of the posse look to Holton and Jules seated against the wall. Sheriff Lowe then glances at their meager provisions. "With our horses and gear gone, what're we gonna eat?"

Staring at the man, Holton rests his rifle across his knee. "You ain't *captives*, you're free to go." When the sheriff looks to the pile of weapons, Holton adds, "Without guns, of course."

Jules drinks from a canteen and passes it over to Holton. The sheriff licks his lips and grumbles, "What about *water*?"

After taking a swallow from the canteen, Holton lifts the rifle barrel and points. "There's a river down below a ways…"

As Holton sets the canteen down, the sheriff crosses his arms and sits back. "You'll *hang* fer this, Lang."

"You've said *that* before."

"I'll *see to it* that it *gits done.*"

Holton notices Jules going through the weapons, loading each gun with rounds from discarded cartridge belts. He turns back to the sheriff and shrugs. "Sheriff... I think you've got more important matters to see to first."

~*~

Standing on a wooden crate, Bear attaches a canvas cover to an old military supply wagon. Ernesto sorts through the wagon-team harnesses, inspecting the leather for any necessary repairs. Behind them, Alice comes from the cabin with an armful of supplies. She strides over and places them near the back of the wagon. As Bear struggles with pulling the large canvas over the wagon's canopy ribs, Alice inquires, "When will we be ready to go?"

Bear stops what he's doing to stare down at her. "*We...?* Where d'ya think *yer* goin'?"

Alice meets his stare. "*With* you."

Stupefied, Bear sputters, "The *hell* you say..."

She gives the grizzled scout a stern look, glances over to Ernesto and then at Dog sitting nearby in the shade. The canine whimpers and lowers his head to the ground, as she declares, "*I sure as heck ain't staying behind to have this baby alone.*"

Bear points at Ernesto. "*He* can stay with ya..."

The Mexican instantly drops what he's doing, shakes his head and waves both hands. "No, Señor... I no make the baby, and I no bring the baby into this world."

Bewildered, Bear spouts, "Well, *hellfire…! I* didn't make the baby, *neither.*"

Alice smooths the apron over her rounded midsection and starts to walk back toward the cabin. "Stop your belly-achin', the *both* of ya. I'm going along, and that's the *end* of it." Midway, she stops and turns to look back at Bear. Standing atop the wagon, he scratches his chin and timidly looks away. Her stern visage travels to Ernesto, who drops his gaze and returns to his task. Finally, she looks to Dog, who lets out a low whine before lying down submissively. Satisfied, she rests her hands on her hips and addresses the lot of them. "Very good… Now that it's all understood, *when* do we *leave?*"

Lifting his hat to scratch the back of his head, Bear peers over at the horses in the corral. "I should think first thing tomorrow mornin' will be 'bout right."

"That's fine… I'll gather the rest of our travel supplies, and we will depart at first light." Bear goes back to the job of attaching the canvas awning to the wagon, while grumbling a few choice words under his breath. Almost to the cabin, Alice stops, clears her throat, and directs another stare at him. "*Excuse me?* What was that, Mister Benton?" He turns to receive her hard look, as she adds, "Speak *up,* if you'd like to be *heard.*"

"Oh, nothin'… Jest remindin' myself again what a *joy* this's gonna be, and how ol' *Holton Lang* is the cause of it all." Taking a deep breath, Alice pats the front of her skirt and turns to go back inside, while Bear continues to mutter, "Holton... I'm gonna git ya *back* fer this one day!"

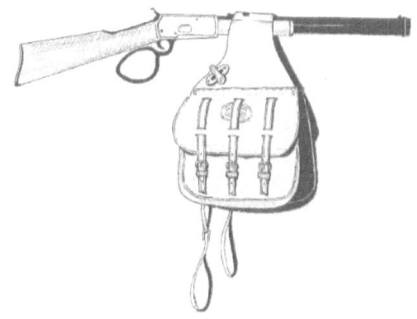

Chapter 29

Jules and Holton are positioned at the rear wall of the ruins, within easy reach of the pile of firearms and cartridge belts. Waiting for an opportunity, the three surviving posse members lie low against the front wall of stacked rocks.

Sheriff Lowe peers out through a small window opening and then turns back to address Holton. "Hey Lang... Ya think them Injuns are gone from here yet?"

"Go see for yerself."

The sheriff nudges the injured man next to him to raise his hat up above the rock wall. An arrow zings through the hat's crown and rattles off the stone wall across the way. Bringing his hat down to his lap, the man inspects the new hole. He looks to the sheriff, and then to his companion with the stub of an arrow still poking out of his head. "Damn, I should've used *his* hat, since it already has a hole in it."

As the man with the head wound reaches up and tries, unsuccessfully, to wobble the firmly stuck shaft free, the annoyed sheriff sighs. "Cripes…"

Staring at the man with the arrow in his skull, Jules scoots closer to Holton. "How is it that he has that thing stuck in his head, and it didn't *kill* him?"

"Some folks don't use what's inside as much as others."

Jules smiles and shakes his head. "Yeah, I guess so… Hard to believe until you see it."

"Get some sleep, and I'll wake you when I get tired."

"How long will we stay?"

Holton thinks on it a moment. "Until our hunger builds-up our courage enough to leave…"

~*~

The morning sky is just starting to brighten, as the supply wagon rolls down the ranch lane and through the gate. Bear drives the rig, and the pregnant woman sits beside him. Coming along behind, Ernesto rides one of the saddled mounts, and Dog trots along beside.

The odd mix of travellers keeps quiet, each thinking of what lies ahead as they attempt the rescue of Holton and Jules. Alice holds a hand over her swollen belly to support the baby. Ernesto rides with a sense of loyalty, and Bear spits to the side, ruminating about how, someday, he'll get even. As the dust settles, the cabin at the ranch sits vacant. Ambling past the barn, a

Del Rio Hondo

lone cow walks toward the dwelling, then up the hill past the recently constructed foundation of the unfinished home.

~*~

The sheriff and what's left of his posse sit hunched against the rock wall, hungry and very thirsty. Disheartened, they stare at each other, aimlessly waiting. A short distance away from them, Jules sits watching with a pistol in his lap. Holton walks across the chamber, looks outside and listens. Turning to the sheriff and his men, he notices that one of the deceased is starting to swell in the heat. "We need to get the dead ones out of here, before they get to stinkin' so bad we can't stand it."

The sheriff glares at Holton, tries to spit, but doesn't have the saliva to do it. With a dry throat, he croaks, "Yeah? And, where are we s'posed to bury 'em?"

"I didn't say you had to bury 'em..."

The sheriff kicks his heels into the stone floor and then peeks out over the rock wall. An arrow whizzes over his head, and he quickly ducks down. "Those bastards..." He looks over to Holton and grumbles, "What d'ya suggest we do with 'em?"

Holton swishes the nearly empty canteen he's been sharing with Jules, looks to the young man and sets it aside. Turning back to the sheriff, he offers, "Heave 'im over the side."

Shocked by the suggestion, the sheriff tries to swallow, but just coughs. *"Jest let 'em tumble down the rocks?"*

"Better they smell him down there than us up here."

The sheriff and his men look at their dead companions and wince at the stinking odor coming from the corpse that is already swelling. Holton sniffs the foul air, pinches his nose and shakes his head. "He ain't gonna get any better."

Resentful, but acceptant, the sheriff motions for his men to help him do the deed. When they touch the swollen body, some of the stretched skin begins to sluff off. Carefully, they grip the man by his clothing and lift him up to the top of the crumbling rock wall.

Choking back the rising bile from his empty stomach, the sheriff tries not to take in the stench of the dead body. "Okay, boys... *Heave-ho...*"

Retching at the awful smell, they push the limp form over the wall, and it tumbles down the rocky escarpment. When the corpse hits the first big rock, the body splits open. With a hiss of gas, it breaks apart before it reaches the bottom. The noxious odor catches on the afternoon breeze and travels up to the cliff dwelling. They all hold their hands over their noses and mouth to block the stench that wafts over them. Coughing, the sheriff grumbles, "Crimey...! That feller stinks worse than when he was *alive.*"

Settling back into waiting, everyone tries not to breathe in the smell or think about their dire situation. They all watch, as circling carrion birds flap down and land to pick at the bits of scattered remains. One of the men from the posse speaks up. "Ya think that might've scared-off them Injuns?"

Sheriff Lowe slowly turns to give him a glowering stare. "Well, why don't you jest go down

Del Rio Hondo

there and see for yerself…" The man sheepishly hunkers back down against the low wall, while the sheriff continues to watch Holton and Jules relax in the shade at the back of the dwelling.

Chapter 30

Watching the trail attentively, Alice drives the wagon team, as Bear walks on ahead with Dog. His eyes cast skyward, Ernesto rides up alongside the wagon. Alice glances over at him and follows his gaze up to the circling birds.

Ahead, Dog stops at a cluster of brush, lowers his head, growls, and looks at Bear. The old cavalry scout covers his nose with his neckerchief to mask a terrible stench. Looking up to the buzzards overhead, he sees one swoop down and land close to some distant cliff dwellings. Then, following Dog's lead, Bear investigates behind the shrubs and finds a dead body. Swollen from days in the sun, the features of the man are unrecognizable. Bear looks at the dog and shakes his head. "Dog, ya found another one." Then, to himself, he mutters, "One hell of a trail they left…"

Dog steps closer, points his nose out and gives a low whimper. Looking back at the body, Bear notices sunlight shimmering on the handle of a holstered pistol. He moves in, pulls the sidearm out and gives it a good looking-over. Nodding his head, he turns to Dog and then looks back at the fancily engraved pistol. "Dang… Yer right as the rain, y'are… This is the same shooter the kid carried."

Alice pulls back on the reins to halt the team, as Ernesto stops his mount. Holding a hand against the tiny kicks she feels in her belly, Alice breaks into a nervous sweat. Anticipating bad news, she calls out to Bear. "Dog found *another* one…?"

Bear palms the handgun and walks to the wagon. "Yep…" He steps alongside the wagon and places Jules' gun in the driver's box at Alice's feet. "He weren't one of our'n, but he was carryin' the boy's gun."

Alice lets her gaze drift back up to the circling buzzards and then looks down to Bear. "You think they're still alive?"

Bear shrugs. "Holton is orn'ry… A tough one to kill… Believe me, many've tried, but he usually comes out okay." Concerned, Alice rubs her hand over her belly. Bear continues, "Don't you worry, ma'am. We'll keep lookin' 'til we find 'em." He motions for her to scoot over and then climbs up beside her. He takes hold of the reins and gives them a slap. Ernesto follows the wagon, and Dog trots off ahead.

~*~

Eric H. Heisner

The group taking shelter in the cliff dwelling is dehydrated, and hungry. Holton and Jules sit opposite the posse, motionless, waiting for the hottest part of the day to pass. When he hears rocks faintly crunching underfoot as someone approaches, Jules nudges Holton. Holding his handgun ready, he whispers, "Holton... I thought those Apache were afraid to come up here?

Straining to hear, Holton lifts the barrel of his rifle and clicks back the hammer. "Some of them are more superstitious than others..."

The sheriff and his men can tell that Holton and Jules are readying for an attack. In a low, dry voice, the sheriff pleads, "Give us our guns."

Holton shakes his head. "There's only a few..."

Suddenly, a canine trots through the doorway and scans his dark eyes around the chamber. Relieved, Jules blurts, "Dog...! How'd ya find us?" The canine displays recognition and then steps aside, as Bear and Ernesto, sweating and heaving for breath, enter the room.

Holton lowers the aim of his rifle and stares at them. "What are the two of you doing *here?*"

As he tries to catch his breath, Bear looks around the carved-out room and then looks back outside to the view. "Well, *that's* a fine greetin' for us comin' to yer rescue..."

Holding his wound, Holton weakly gets to his feet and then stumbles against the wall. "If you're both *here*, where did you leave the *woman?*"

Obliging, Ernesto points outside to the wagon below. "She's down there, waiting."

Del Rio Hondo

Holton walks over, looks out and sees the horse-drawn wagon "You brought her *with* you?"

Bear grunts. "It's not like I had a choice in the matter."

Holton is aghast. "She's gonna have a *baby* soon."

"Yeah… I *noticed!*"

Cradling his rifle over his arm, Holton shakes his head, as he looks toward Sheriff Lowe and his two remaining men. "It's not safe for her here…"

Bear follows Holton's gaze to the posse. "It warn't too safe back at the ranch neither."

"What about the ones they left to watch over you?"

The gruff scout spits to the side and wipes his chin. "Let's jest say that squatter graveyard of yourn jest got a couple more added."

Ernesto hands his canteen over to Jules who drinks. Holton turns to look at them and offers, "Don't drink too much, or you'll get sick." Jules stops and offers Holton the canteen. When one of the posse members reaches out for it, Dog growls, and the man quickly pulls his hand back. Holton downs a mouthful, and hands the canteen back to Ernesto. Holton asks, "How'd they get *you* to come along?"

Ernesto slings the canteen over his shoulder, puffs his chest out and stands proudly. "They could not stop *me*, either."

Holton turns to Bear and, under his breath, grumbles, "Great… Got the whole merry band now."

After taking a swig from his own canteen, Bear looks around the room again. "We found most of what's left from your encounter with the locals."

Holton turns his gaze to the sheriff's posse, and the men shift apprehensively. Sheriff Lowe sits up and dryly croaks, "What're ya gonna do with us now?"

"We're taking you along with us."

Bear scratches his beard. "Back to the ranch...?"

Holton shakes his head and looks out to the waiting wagon down below. "No... Back to Texas."

Chapter 31

That evening, the wagon sits close to the cliff wall, hidden from the rest of the valley. Standing next to a small fire, Holton and Jules are feeling much better with Alice's cooking in them. Bound to a wagon-wheel, the sheriff and his men eat meager portions from a shared plate. Bear comes from the rear of the wagon and looks down at them. Then, he looks to those by the campfire and grunts, "Holton... I still think it's a real bad idea takin' these fellers all the way back to Texas."

Noticing the woman's look of concern, Holton suggests, "If we don't deal with them now, there'll be others later."

Sitting down next to Ernesto, Jules remains quiet, and Bear looks at him. "Ya think that's right, boy?"

The young man looks up at Bear and nods. "They done some real bad things already and won't stop till they hang us and git what they want."

Alice looks over at the prisoners. "Let's get it over and done with before this baby comes along."

Everyone looks to the woman's bulging midsection. In the flickering light, Holton tries to make out her expression. "We'll be passing through a friendly village near Fort Stanton. We could leave you there, while we finish our business."

"I'll be going wherever *you* go."

Not wanting to argue with her, Holton looks to Bear. "How're *you* feelin', pard?"

The scout stretches, and touches where his old wound has healed. "*I* ain't staying behind, *neither.*"

Holton turns to Ernesto. The Mexican smiles and offers, "I, too, come along where you go, Señor."

Overruled, Holton shakes his head and turns to Jules. "Hey, kid. I guess we'll have some company along on this one."

Jules speaks with a sly grin. "I know a nice family with a ranch where we could probably stay a spell..."

~*~

The morning sun casts long shadows across the cliffs. The wagon, packed, and the team hitched, is ready to depart. Bear carefully straightens out a set of harness lines and then looks to the pair of saddled mounts tied to nearby bushes. Moving to the front of the wagon, he reaches into the driver's box and grabs the engraved pistol he found on the dead man. "Hey, Jules... C'mere a minute..."

Del Rio Hondo

Leaving Ernesto to guard the sheriff and his two men, Jules comes from the rear of the wagon. "Yes, sir?"

Bear blows on the fancy pistol and holds it out to him. "Thought ya might like this back…"

Jules looks down at the gun, and then pulls a plain, walnut-handled six-shooter from his holster. "Thank you. How'd ya find it?"

Bear tilts his head to where the dog sits watching them. "Dog, there, found it."

Jules looks to the dog and smiles. He takes the fancy gun, spins it on a finger and drops it into his cartridge-belt holster. Holding the extra gun, Jules asks, "What do I do with this one?"

The scout gestures to the pair of saddled horses nearby. "Slip 'er in the saddlebag, if ya got room. N'er know when ya might have use fer it."

Jules looks at the horses. "Which one do I get?"

"Whichever of 'em ya git to first, I reckon. Although… I'd leave the taller one fer Holton."

The young man eyes the horses and turns back to Bear. "Thank you, Mister Benton."

He pats Jules kindly on the arm. "You jest call me Bear, like everyone else."

"Thanks, Bear."

"Ya earned it, kid. Me 'nd Ernie there will stay in the wagon with the woman 'nd keep those fellers under a close eye. You and Holton will need to scout ahead."

With a nod, Jules walks over to the shorter of the two horses and inspects the cinch for tightness. He slips the extra pistol into the saddle pouch and sees that there is a long-gun tucked in each saddle's rifle scabbard.

157

Conspicuously, Holton's big-loop rifle is in the other sheath. Tossing a smile back to Bear, Jules mounts up.

Mounting the taller horse, Holton notices the fancy pistol in Jules' holster. With a twinkle in his eye, Holton says, "Jest like old times, eh, kid?"

Jules can't help but flash a grin, as he looks back at the others in the wagon. "Almost…"

Carrying a double-barreled shotgun, Ernesto climbs into the back of the wagon to guard the prisoners. The riders watch Bear climb into the driver's seat and take the lines from Alice. The old cavalry scout waves onward and gives the reins a slap. The team steps up and the creaking wagon rolls forward. Holton turns in the saddle and stares in the direction of Texas. "Yeah… Almost…"

Chapter 32

Riding ahead of the wagon, Holton and Jules follow Dog's lead on the path eastward. The dust kicked up by the wagon drifts on the afternoon breeze. As the long days of travel drag on, the prisoners, under constant guard, remain ever watchful for an opportunity to turn the tables.

Rocking with the motion of the wagon, Sheriff Lowe watches Ernesto, across from him, fight the urge to drift off. One of the men is about to reach for the shotgun, but the sheriff stops him with a whisper. "Not yet…"

Confused, the posse member stops to look at the sheriff. "Why the hell *not…?*"

"We're nearly back to Texas."

"*So...?*"

"They're *takin'* us jest where we want 'em to *go*."

"Yeah, but as *pris'ners...*"

The sheriff looks outside through a canvas flap and lowers his voice even more. "We try to take 'em now, they'll scatter like goats." He looks to see Ernesto still struggling to stay awake and continues, "On home turf, we'll have the numbers on our side."

The hiss of their whispering jolts Ernesto awake. "Señor... You be quiet there."

Sheriff Lowe smiles pleasantly at the sleepy Mexican. "Jest talkin' 'bout the weather..."

"Que...?"

"There's a storm a'comin'..."

Ernesto looks out the rear of the wagon to see a clear western sky. "Looks like blue skies to me."

Lowe looks over at his man and gives a broad wink. "This one you won't see comin'..."

From the front, Bear peeks into the wagon bed and skillfully hits the sheriff's boot with a spit of tobacco juice. "Now *hush,* back there... We don't need no *guff* from ya." Clenching his jaw, the sheriff looks down at the spittle dripping of his foot. He holds his tongue, as Bear faces forward and gives a slap of the reins.

Ernesto notices the sheriff and his pair of men exchanging looks. With his thumb on the pulled back hammers, he holds his shotgun tightly to his chest.

~*~

On the outskirts of the village of Rio Hondo, Holton and Jules wait for the supply wagon to catch up.

160

Del Rio Hondo

As they lead their party down the empty main street, they are greeted by cautious eyes peeking out from windows and doorways. Ernesto jumps from the back of the wagon and walks up front next to the harness team. "The people are afraid."

Bear glances back at the prisoners and then looks down to Ernesto. "Why would that be?"

The Mexican looks up at Bear. "The last time Señor Lang was in town, there was a great fight."

Looking to Alice beside him and then nodding in agreement, Bear snorts, "Yeah... He does seem to have that effect on a place." He glances back at the sheriff in the wagon and then nudges the rifle prudently set between him and Alice. "Until we git settled in, best to keep an eye on 'em back there." She takes the rifle, levers it, and points the gun at the prisoners. Relaxing to the sway of the rolling wagon, they return her stare.

At the end of the street, Ernesto points to a group of buildings north of town. "That is where many of my family live. It is a small farm, but there should be a warm meal ready for us at most any time."

Slowing their mounts to ride alongside the wagon, Holton exchanges a glance with Jules and then looks to the smiling Mexican. "That would be fine. Anything would beat *Bear's* cookin'..." Jules laughs and follows Holton as they ride after the Mexican villager returned home.

As they approach the farmstead, several people come out of an adobe house to welcome them. Ernesto greets them. "Hello, Mama y Papa! See here who I have brought." Uncertain, they first look at Holton and then to

Eric H. Heisner

Bear, driving the wagon, and to Alice, holding the rifle. Their gaze finally falls on Jules and the gun strapped to his side. Ernesto joins them, and they converse in whispered Spanish. Offended by what they say, he speaks back to them in an admonishing tone.

Stopping the team, Bear exchanges a glance with Holton and then Alice. "Seems we ain't as welcome as he thought..." Lowering the rifle to her lap, Alice tries to appear less hostile. Suddenly, a pang of abdominal cramping grips her. She lets go of the gun and clutches her belly. Alarmed, Bear turns to her. *"You okay there, missy?!?"*

"Just some contracting pains..."

"You gonna have the baby *now?"*

Alice blows out a lungful of air and shakes her head. "No...Too early yet... It'll pass."

All eyes are on her, as she breathes through the pain. Ernesto and his family stop talking and rush over to help Alice down from the wagon. The cautious reception shifts to a welcoming one as Alice is ushered into the home.

Holton dismounts and Jules holds his mount as he unsheathes his big loop rifle before walking over to the wagon. Looking up at Bear, Holton asks, "What's wrong with her?"

Bear looks to the doorway of the farmhouse and shrugs. "I 'spect she could be havin' that baby anytime."

"She shouldn't have come along."

"Yer preachin' to the choir, brother..."

Holton shakes his head, glances at the family's house, and then looks to Jules as he secures their horses near the barn. He looks back to Bear. "How are our guests faring?"

Bear looks into the wagon and lets out an irritated groan. At the rear of the wagon, Holton pulls back the canvas flap and reveals an empty bed. He turns and looks around, but there is no sign of the sheriff or his men.

Bear curses. *"Damn…"*

Staring at Bear across the empty wagon, Holton inquires, "How long they been gone?"

"Could be since we passed through that village."

"So much for our surprise return…"

Bear nods and looks down to the empty spot where Alice's rifle was dropped. "Yeah… They got a *rifle* now, too."

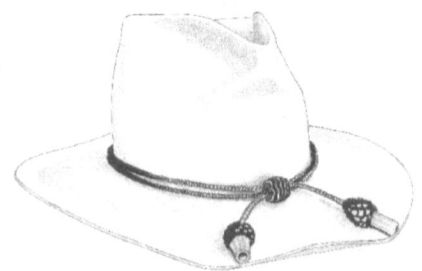

Chapter 33

The next morning, as Holton and Jules saddle their horses, Bear walks over from the farmhouse. Scratching his beard, he grumbles, "Why'd I let ya convince me to stay with her *again?*"

Holton look over and fastens the flap on his saddlebag. "It's best for everyone."

Bear protests, "Not for *me*, it ain't!"

Mounting, Jules looks over to Bear. "Holton can stay, and I can go on alone."

The two old friends exchange a look and Holton tilts his head toward the youngster. "See what I have to deal with?" Bear nods in agreement, then steps back as Holton mounts. "With us gone, no one should bother you here."

Del Rio Hondo

Bear reaches out and takes a firm hold of Holton's leg. "This is the *last* time I let ya run off 'nd leave me behind with the womenfolk."

"You're still healing up."

Looking at the dried blood on Holton's shirt, he snorts, "Heck... You've been shot a hell of a lot more recent than *me*."

Shifting the reins between his fingers, Holton peers down at his friend. "Jest keep her here awhile, if you can."

"*Hellfire*, I'd rather be goin' along with the both of *you*." He removes his hand from Holton's leg and waves him off.

Holton backs his horse and turns east, toward Texas. "Thanks, pard... I owe ya one."

Holton and Jules ride away, and Dog trails after them. Bear hollers, "Holton...! You owe me *two!!!*

~*~

Days later, Holton and Jules halt their horses on the high ground overlooking Francisco's homestead. All is quiet. Not a horse or person in sight... Jules looks at Holton questioningly. "Where are they? I don't see anyone down there."

"Yeah, a mite more peaceable than the last time we come upon this place..." Beside them, Dog sits on his haunches, silently scanning from the ranch buildings over to the creek. Holton looks down at the canine. "What do you think, Dog?" The dog barks once, then stands and trots down the slope toward the house and barn. Holton and Jules exchange a glance before prodding their horses forward.

Eric H. Heisner

After checking inside the barn, Holton watches Jules ride around the sod house. When they meet at the corral fence, Holton shakes his head. "Barn's empty... Find anyone?"

"Nope."

Holton looks to the late afternoon sun and dismounts. "We'll spend the night here and look for any tellin' signs of them in the morning."

Gazing around the once-welcoming homestead, Jules feels a deep sense of remorse. "I should've *stayed* with them."

"Regret will get you nothing but muddled thoughts."

"They're probably dead."

Holton turns his gaze toward the small family graveyard by the water. "I only see one fresh grave..."

A knot sticks in Jules' throat at the thought of young William's death, and he tries to swallow it. Clenching his jaw to keep from crying, he looks around the vacant ranch yard. "They've all been run off then."

Holton reaches under his stirrup and undoes the saddle's cinch. "Possible..." He looks over to see Jules gazing toward the empty house. When the cinch strap dangles loose, Holton pulls the saddle off the horse and drapes it over the top rail of the fence. He unties his bedroll from behind the saddle cantle and turns to consider the overnight accommodations. "House or barn tonight? Yer pick..."

Still lost in his feelings, Jules turns his horse. "Holton... It don't feel right setting up inside their home with them gone. Let's stay in the barn."

Del Rio Hondo

"Fine by me." With his rifle in one hand and the bedroll and saddlebags in the other, Holton walks to the mud-brick barn and swings both doors open wide. He looks back at Jules, as the young man somberly dismounts and starts to unsaddle. Deep down, he knows the sorrow Jules must be feeling, and he ponders on the special bond that has developed between them because of his commitment to guide the boy into manhood.

~*~

Several miles away, the sheriff and what's left of his posse ride into Big Spring, Texas looking haggard after their long ordeal. They quietly ride down the main street toward the train yard at the far end of town.

In front of the office near the multiple tracks of iron rail that converge next to the depot, the three riders dismount. Sheriff Lowe directs his men to care for the borrowed horses. Then, with heavy, determined steps, he walks up the stairs to the boardwalk and into the railroad baron's headquarters.

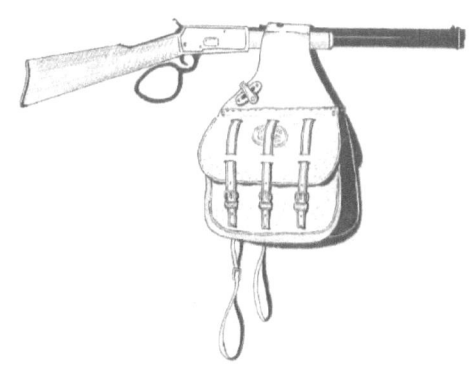

Chapter 34

Holton and Jules raise a trail of dust, as they leave the deserted homestead and ride toward the rising sun. With a watchful eye on the horizon, they scan the ground ahead for any sign of noticeable tracks.

~*~

At his desk, Colonel Jackson Henry writes a message on a piece of paper. He signs the letter and looks up at the sheriff standing before him. Washed-up, rested and freshly laundered, the lawman is respectfully presentable. "Sheriff, I trust a night's sleep has put you in a more *civil* frame of mind?"

The sheriff nods, as he glances out the window at the typical activity in the street. He looks back to the colonel. "Feelin' better, thanks."

As he hands the paper to the sheriff, the colonel offers, "I just posted this reward for Holton Lang and the boy, Jules." He watches the sheriff read it over. "I want you to get the message out to every cowboy looking to make a few dollars. We'll scour every inch of ground from here to Arizona."

The lawman lowers the paper to stare at the gentleman behind the desk. "No need to be searchin' *that* far... Last I knew, they were on their way here to meet with you."

The chair creaks, as the colonel leans back and folds his hands in his lap. "Did they say *where* they'd like to meet?"

"I imagine they'll be out at the Garcia place."

The colonel smiles. "It's not their home anymore."

Not too surprised, the sheriff asks, "What happened? Did ya have him killed?"

"Let's just say. They abandoned it for greener pastures."

The sheriff takes another look at the letter and, with regard to the reward, shakes his head. "With this amount of money on their heads, we'll have every low-life in the territory chasin' after 'em."

"You'll still get your money, Sheriff..."

"There was no doubt 'bout that... It's jest that there'll be a lot of extra folks comin' 'round to take into account."

Del Rio Hondo

His chair squeaking as it rocks, the colonel shrugs. "What's a few more sacrificial targets to make it easier for you and your men to complete the task...?"

"I don't know..."

"You don't have to *know* anything. This is what I *want*."

"It could git messy."

The colonel puts his hands together, intertwines his fingers and leans forward on his desk. "It's *already* been messy. Now, it's time to clean things up." The sheriff folds the paper, puts it in his pocket, nods and exits the office.

~*~

Reaching an embankment with a view over the river, Holton and Jules spot a few loose cattle scattered on the far side. Jules identifies the markings of the family brand and confirms, "Those are Garcia cattle, all right."

Holton twists himself in the saddle to look around. "From the way things look 'round here, he's not much better of a cattleman than I am."

Defensive at the critical remark, Jules snaps at Holton. "He's *really* good at using a rope."

Breaking from his survey of the terrain, Holton notices the boy's concern. "No offense meant to his ranching skills." Looking again to the scattered longhorns, he thinks of his own unattended spread in Arizona. "Kid, I'm just referring to his not being present to watch over his animals. I have a similar situation with Charlie Nichols' herd."

"Mister Garcia was a good and generous man."

"He seemed to be..."

171

The two stare silently for a while. Finally, Jules wipes a finger under his eye and clears his throat. "He had a family to take care of."

"It's a big responsibility."

The young man states, "They're alive yet... I *know* it."

Holton notices that there is more that Jules wants to say but doesn't pry. "Could be..." Holton pulls his horse's head up from grazing and adjusts his reins. "We'll head into Big Spring tomorrow and see what this colonel has to say about things."

Jules is surprised. "You want to *talk* with him?"

"I don't think just killing him would solve much."

"*I* do."

"There might be a way to work things out yet."

Skeptical, Jules shakes his head. "He'll hang us, for sure. He had *no* qualms about lynching a young boy."

Taking the thought into consideration, Holton nods. "You can hold back at the Garcia place if you'd like. It'll be better to be in town, out in the open than to have a mob of hired guns pin us down at the ranch."

Holton backs his horse away from the embankment, and Jules turns his horse to follow. "I'll stick close to you, Holton. It's just that these men can't be trusted."

"Sad truth is, the ones in charge often can't be."

From the riverbank, the two ride back in the direction of the Garcia homestead.

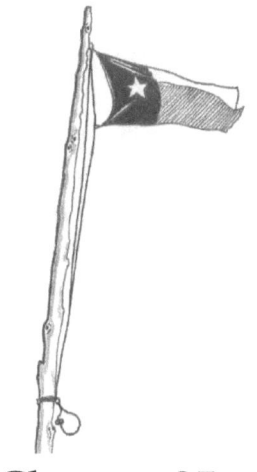

Chapter 35

With his daughter beside him and leading a horse that carries his wife, Francisco Garcia approaches a small encampment of weather-stained canvas structures near Colorado City, Texas. At first glance, the rough-looking men living there could be taken to be a gang of hardened outlaws. Closer inspection reveals that a few of the better-dressed ones wear small, handmade, cinco peso Texas Ranger badges. Nervously studying the men in the camp, Fransisco discerns several inhospitable faces among them. "This is a bad idea…"

Holding her father's hand, Alejandra gives it a squeeze. "No, Papa… Jules said to me that the rangers are *good* men."

"Not from the stories *I* have heard." Curious, he turns to look at his daughter. "*Jules...?* I think it is *Mister Ward* to *you*."

She blushes and argues, "I am nearly his age."

"Not hardly..."

"Oh, Father... He is not as old as he seems, and I am near the age to get married."

Looking around the ranger camp, Francisco grimaces. "Please stop this talk of marriage. One problem at a time..."

She hugs closer to her father's side. "We are in the right. I think these men could help us."

"I think I should have left you and your mother behind and come here alone."

"You said these men would try to lynch you."

He nods. "They still might."

"Just for asking for their help...?"

"The Tejas Rangers have done a lot worse to the people of our color for much less."

Hard looks from the rangers abound, as the group walks up to the camp. A gruff man, with a badge pinned to his vest and a rifle held at the ready, greets them. "Hold it there, Mexican... What's yer business here?"

Francisco pushes his daughter behind him and removes his hat. "Greetings, Señor... I am *Spanish*, and we are here to ask for the help of the Texas Rangers."

The ranger chuckles, revealing a big, gap-toothed grin. He turns to those watching them from the camp and hollers, "Hey, boys...! Listen to this. This here *Mexican* wants our *help!*"

Del Rio Hondo

A ranger loafing by a small cook fire points south and snaps back, "Tell 'im that Ol' Mexico is in *that* direction." Several men hoot, while the others just ignore the discussion.

With another heartening squeeze from his daughter's hand, Francisco glances at her, then stands tall and asks, "Please, sir, can I talk with the gentleman who is the leader? There is a very bad person in Big Spring, not too far from here, who is taking our land by force."

"Sorry, Mex... This land belongs to Texas now."

"Señor, I bought land with money I earn in Tejas."

Lowering his rifle, the ranger looks to the young daughter and then to Francisco's wife. "Trust me... You'd be better-off headin' south."

Holding his temper, Francisco shakes his head. "Could I *please* speak with someone?"

"We got nothin' for ya, Mexican."

"I told you... I am *Spanish*."

Irritated, the Texas Ranger holds firm. He grumbles, "Whatever you are, you don't understand English too well..."

Alejandra grips her father's arm and whispers in his ear. "Tell him about Jules."

Francisco glances at her briefly, sighs, and then looks back to the guard. "There is a young white man, *Señor Ward*, who was helping us, and was taken by people in Big Spring." At the mention of a familiar name, a passing ranger stops.

The guard raises his rifle broadside to push Francisco back, stating, "Sorry, Hombre. We cain't help."

"Are you not men of the law?"

"Not for *Mexicans*..."

The insult is too much for Francisco, and he cannot control his anger any longer. He removes his daughter from his arm, throws down his hat, takes a fighting stance and raises his fists. "You call me a Mexican *one more time*..."

Smiling, the ranger turns his rifle, puts it to his shoulder and aims it at Francisco. "You *really* wanna play this game?"

The Spaniard holds his ground and braces himself to fight. "I will *not* be insulted in front of my wife and daughter by some *dirty gringo* with a *badge*."

The camp guard clicks back the hammer on his rifle. "Whatever you *say*, Mexi..."

Before the insult is completed, a Texas Ranger steps up from behind the guard and swats the rifle barrel away. Francisco is about to lunge forward, but the intervening ranger holds out his hand. "Hold on, now!" Francisco freezes, the guard lowers his aim and Ranger Hobbs assesses the situation. "What's goin' on here?"

"Just doing my job, sir."

Hobbs nods to the guard and gestures toward the rifle. "Uncock that rifle..."

"But, sir..."

"We don't shoot men in a fist fight..." Hobbs looks toward Francisco. "Despite our reputations."

Bewildered, the guard eases-down the hammer of his rifle and looks to his superior officer. "Sir...?"

Del Rio Hondo

Ranger Hobbs looks beyond them to Alejandra and her mother. "Were you gonna to shoot *them*, too?"

"No, sir..."

Ranger Hobbs turns to address Francisco and his family. "What's the problem here?"

Taking a deep, calming breath, Francisco picks up his hat and reclaims his modest demeanor. "We thank you, Señor. We are in desperate need of your help."

Hobbs nods and glances to the men watching from camp. "Yeah, I heard *that* part already. What of this *gringo* boy you mentioned? Mister *Ward...?*"

Alejandra's eyes light up. She steps forward and blurts, "Jules is a brave man, who helped us when others would not."

Hobbs turns his attention to her. "Jules?"

"Sí."

"I'll be damned... Was he riding with an ugly dog and a man wearin' fringed buckskin?"

"Sí, that is correct! But, the man and dog have gone away, and Jules is in much trouble."

Hobbs cracks a smile and waves for them to follow him. "I know some about this Señor Ward and his friend's doin's. Come with me, and we can talk." Nearly tripping over his large-roweled spurs, Ranger Hobbs walks toward a row of less-worn canvas wall-tents. Francisco shrugs to his family, grabs the horse's lead lines and follows.

Chapter 36

Leaving the ranch, Holton and Jules head in the direction of town. Jules pushes his horse to keep pace with Holton's mount. Catching up, he speaks his mind. "Holton, I still don't think this is a good idea…"

The westerner glances over at the youth and nods. "There aren't a lot of options to pick from."

"We find where he lives and ride out to his place."

"Then what…?"

"We set things right."

Holton notices Dog, trotting ahead of them, sniff the air. "Who are we to say what's right?"

Jules, haunted by the image of the young boy hanging in the barn, clenches his jaw. "They killed William."

"This man in charge did that?"

"No... But, he's responsible."

Soon, the town of Big Spring appears on the horizon. When closer, they notice that there are an awful lot of men, horses, and wagons gathered on the street for such a small town. Holton ponders aloud. "Don't know the day of the week, but everyone seems to have come to do their business today..."

"Maybe it's a market day?"

Dog lets out a low growl, and Holton motions for Jules to follow him toward a set of railroad tracks leading in from the edge of town. "On second thought, let's not ride down the middle of the street."

Skirting the edge of the settlement, they reach the train tracks and follow them in. Riding through a freight yard stacked with boxcars and livestock carriers, Holton and Jules make their way to the rail headquarters adjacent to the tracks. There are several groups of armed men in front of the building, milling about as if waiting for someone.

Concealed behind a rail car, Holton and Jules study the tough crowd. Jules shakes his head and rests his hand on the grip of his pistol. "Not very inviting..."

Holton looks to Dog nearby, then to Jules watching him, and dismounts. "Let's leave the horses here."

Jules steps down and lets his reins drop to the ground. "I think we'd have a better chance against them at the ranch."

Holton draws his rifle out of the saddle scabbard and quietly levers a round into the chamber. "We'll see if we can get an audience with the colonel without disturbing the hive."

Dog whines softly and lies down, as Jules lifts his pistol in the holster, readying for an easy pull. He looks back at the canine and then follows Holton's lead.

~*~

Inside the railroad office, Colonel Jackson Henry paces in front of a detailed wall map. He turns to Rickter and another man whose tiny glasses lend him to an academic appearance. The colonel points to the map. "We have all the land rights secured along the waterway…" His gaze turns to the engineer. "How soon can we lay track?"

The gentleman removes his glasses and wipes them on a handkerchief from his vest pocket. He studies the map before addressing the colonel. "The plans are drawn up, but we are yet to get the official land survey for the Garcia tract."

The colonel turns to his man. "How goes it, Rickter?"

"We have a survey crew together, headin' out there now. We should be able to lay track soon."

"I want to have this route operable by year's end."

Rickter nods. "Should be doable."

"Any hangups…?"

Suddenly, they are interrupted by the door bursting open. Turning, they instantly recognize Jules but not Holton. Unshaken by the intrusion, the colonel addresses the youth. "Well, hello, Mister Ward… We were just about to discuss the bounty put out on your head. Now... Who is this that has come to collect it?"

Promptly noticing the blood-crusted bullet-hole in Holton's frontier shirt, Rickter moves to draw his sidearm. Turning the aim of his rifle toward him, Holton explains, "Easy... We come to talk peaceable."

The colonel replies, "It doesn't *look* that way."

Staring at the colonel while keeping his rifle aimed at Rickter, Holton steps further into the room. "Tell your man to keep his hand off that shooter, and it will be."

The colonel looks at Rickter and nods. Turning back to Holton, he asks, "Who are you?"

"Holton Lang."

Unable to believe that the man they have been hunting has suddenly arrived, right here, to his office, the colonel tilts his head. "Mister Lang, there are over dozen men in this town that wish they could have met you first. I'm not sure I will pay the bounty for you arriving at my door of your own accord..." Grinning smugly, the colonel pushes back the sides of his coat and places his hands on his hips to display that he is unarmed. "Sheriff Lowe is especially keen to see the two of you again."

With the news of bounty hunters, Holton feels a pang of regret about leaving the home advantage and coming to town. "We come here to talk about ending this whole affair."

Interested, the colonel moves over to the front of the desk and leans his hip to the edge. "I believe we already have what *we* want. What do *you* need out of this?"

"Let us be."

"Is that *all?*"

"Let the Garcia family live in peace. *On their land...*"

The colonel smiles, glances at the stack of papers on his desk and shakes his head at the visitors. "No... Sorry, but we already have plans for the Garcia spread."

Keeping his rifle aimed at Rickter, Holton stares sternly at the colonel. "*Change* 'em..."

The engineer puts his spectacles on and steps up. "Mister, we can't just *change* them. This is the best route."

Holton glances at the suited man. "Go around."

"That would be prohibitively expensive."

Sensing little threat from the bespectacled civilian, Holton turns his attention back to the colonel. "You're gonna have to change your plans."

Lifting his leg to sit on the edge of the desk, the colonel shakes his head. "No... *You* might have to change *yours...*"

Chapter 37

In one swift movement, Jules draws and cocks his pistol. Aiming it at Colonel Henry, he proclaims, "Holton, there's no use talkin' to this man."

Enjoying how quickly the young man loses his temper, Rickter grins wickedly. "Good to see ya again, kid."

Jules turns to Rickter. "I don't feel the same."

"It's too bad it wasn't you I strung up that fine day, and not yer young friend."

Turning the aim of his pistol toward Rickter, Jules fights to keep his emotions in check. "Then, I should kill you now."

In spite of the gun aimed at him, Rickter remains calm. "That day, if we would've run into you and ol'

Del Rio Hondo

Garcia instead, it would've solved a whole lot of our problems."

As Jules' anger wells up, Holton steps between them. "What's it gonna take to put an end to this?"

Perched on the edge of his desk, the colonel crosses his arms and slowly turns his head from side to side. "From where I sit, it doesn't look good for the two of you." Rickter smirks.

Before Jules has a chance to shoot, Holton swings his rifle barrel around to whack Rickter upside the head. The thug tumbles to the floor and then glares up at Holton. "Damn you, Lang! Yer life ain't even worth the bounty that's been offered. I'll *kill* ya myself."

After glancing to Jules, Holton jabs the stock of his rifle into Rickter's face, knocking him out cold. "I just *saved* yours." The rail employee starts for the door and Jules goes after him. When Jules raises his pistol to strike him, the man faints, dropping limply to the floor before the youth can even swing. Jules turns to Holton, who looks down at the unconscious man. "What'd you do that for, kid?"

Just as surprised, Jules answers, "I didn't even hit him."

Knowing where this is going, the colonel leans over to open a desk drawer. He grabs for the derringer inside, but Holton kicks the drawer shut on his hand. He is about to cry out, when he feels the tip of Holton's rifle barrel pressed against his cheek. "You shout, and I shoot."

Painfully, Colonel Henry removes his hand from the drawer and sits up on the desk. "What are you going to do?"

Holton stares at him. "No… What are *you* gonna do?" He grabs the colonel by the collar and drags him off the desk. They move through the room toward the big front window to look outside.

Following, Jules mutters, "What *are* we gonna do…?"

Holton and the colonel see a dozen armed men milling around the hitching rail. Twisting the colonel's collar tighter, Holton hisses in his ear. "What's the army for?"

"They're here to go after *you*."

"Call 'em off."

"I don't think I can… Not without paying them."

Holton turns from the view out the window and looks around the room. "Where do you keep your money?"

"You're going to rob me?"

Jules spots a hidden, wall-safe across the room and pushes a chair blocking it aside. "This is where it is."

Holton pushes the colonel over to it. "Open it."

"I won't."

Examining the large safe, Holton considers his options. Still holding the colonel, he asks, "You keep payroll in there?"

"Yes, and you'll have to kill me before you get it."

Peeking through a window to the alley, Jules has an idea. "Hold on a minute. Be right back…" He slips

Del Rio Hondo

out the same door they just broke in through and quickly returns with a bundle of paper-wrapped sticks bound by a twisted cord.

Confused, Holton asks, "What've you got there, kid?"

The colonel suddenly goes very pale, when Jules grins and guesses, "Dynamite, I think."

Colonel Henry stammers, *"Heavens! D-Don't d-d-do that!* That's enough to level this *entire building!"*

Holton nods his approval and motions Jules to the safe. "Stack it under the hinges."

The colonel watches, horrified. "You light that with us in here, and we'll be blown to bits."

Jules looks back to them after placing the dynamite, and Holton shoves the colonel toward the doorway. "Boy, take him out to our horses. Put him on mine, and I'll take care of this.

Jules stares at Colonel Henry with a burning hatred. "Why…? We should just kill him now and be *done* with it."

With a fatherly demeanor, Holton locks eyes with the youth. "If he gives you *any* trouble at all, you can shoot him." Using his pistol to usher the colonel outside, Jules steps into the alley. Holton follows, dragging the passed-out railroad man.

Keeping his gun poked into the colonel's ribs, Jules looks back to Holton. "What's your plan?"

"Take him to the Garcia place."

Jules gestures to the unconscious man on the stoop. "What about *him?"*

"He'll wake up, eventually."

187

"What'll *you* do?"

"I'm gonna see to it that these bounty hunters get paid, and I'll come join you later." Waving off Jules' look of bewilderment, Holton directs, "Go on, now… And, don't be comin' back. Remember… He balks, shoot him."

"With pleasure."

Jules pushes the colonel down the alleyway toward the railyard where the horses are tied, and Holton goes back into the office. Shortly, Holton returns to unceremoniously dump the unconscious body of Rickter over top of the other man. When he looks down the alley and sees that Jules and the prisoner are clear, Holton returns to the office.

From inside, the scratching sound of a matchstick striking a rough surface. A flame hisses to life, and is then followed shortly by the smashing of a glass lantern.

Chapter 38

Holton steps out through the front door of the railroad office and looks down the main street. The dozen or so men standing around the front of the building all turn to stare curiously, until one of them drops the tobacco plug he was about to cut and stutters, *"Y-Y-You...?!?"*

Holton leaves the door open behind him, as he addresses the crowd. "Your job here is finished, and the fella in charge wants you all to go home."

The man with the tobacco knife comes to his senses and points his small blade at Holton. *"Fellas...* That's *Holton Lang!"* They all stare, dumbfounded, until the man ultimately adds, *"He's* the one the *reward money* is for..."

Eric H. Heisner

One cowboy draws his sidearm and points it at Holton. In a flash, Holton fires his rifle, hitting the man's right arm. Then, he spin-cocks the gun and fans the barrel across the crowd. From the porch, high above the crowd, Holton declares, "The bounty for me and the boy is called-off."

Looking to the wounded man, another one calls out, "We ain't leavin' 'til *someone* gits paid."

As a cloud of smoke starts to billow behind him, Holton glances to the doorway. "You'll be paid what you deserve."

"How's that...?"

"Real soon. We're about to open up the company safe." Holton steps down from the porch, pushes through the crowd to cross the street, and heads for a line of saddled horses.

Stumbling from the back of the building, with a smear of blood running down his face, Rickter calls out to the crowd. "Dammit, boys! That's *him! Kill* 'im...!!"

Without looking back, Holton selects a good horse, unties it and mounts. As he turns the animal to face the crowd, he spots Rickter on the building's front porch and waves him a goodbye salute. Suddenly, as the crowd is about to close in, there is a thundering explosion inside the rail headquarters. The blast shudders through the whole town and the brick wall at the side of the building blows out.

Smoldering bills of currency flutter out over the alleyway and Holton gestures to them. "It's payday, boys..." He spurs his horse and it gallops down the street, as the crowd rushes to collect whatever money can be had.

~*~

Jules leads the horse carrying his bound captive toward the Garcia homestead. As they get near, Jules notices that there are several unfamiliar horses in the corral. Bringing the colonel up alongside him, Jules draws his pistol and pokes it into the man's ribs. The colonel turns to look at Jules and smiles smugly. "Sure doesn't look good, kid. That's probably my survey team."

As Jules counts the horses, he keeps the colonel close. "Just keep riding. Do anything silly, and you'll get a bullet."

Unsure, the man decides to goad the confident teenager. "Those aren't good odds for you. Four to one."

"I've faced worse."

Realizing that the boy is unfazed, the colonel begins to get nervous. "How about you turn me loose now, and I let you hightail it out of here?"

"How 'bout I shoot you *now*?"

"I'll even give you a few bucks to boot."

"Keep riding..."

They approach the barn and a pair of rough characters step outside. Jules slowly cocks back the hammer of his pistol and keeps it steady. Hearing the series of clicks causes the colonel to tense-up, and sweat begins to bead on his forehead. The colonel catches the gaze of the two well-armed men and then looks back to Jules. "What do you want me to do?"

"Say somethin' nice."

The colonel swallows and then calls out. "Take it easy, boys. This fellow has a gun on me."

Chapter 39

Jules is about to speak when he suddenly catches sight of more armed men exiting the sod cabin. One of them addresses him. *"Jules Ward...?"*

Recognizing the voice, Jules turns toward the cabin and squints to identify the man. Relieved, he calls out in return, *"Ranger Hobbs...?"*

Accompanied by Francisco, the ranger walks from the cabin to the barn to join the others. Not recognizing anyone but Garcia, the colonel groans pitifully and slouches in the saddle. Francisco looks first to the colonel and then, with relief, to Jules. "Good to see you, Señor Ward."

Jules returns the greeting. "Good to see you *too,* amigo! You brought the Texas Rangers?"

"Sí, but they come *only* because of *you.*"

Del Rio Hondo

Ranger Hobbs pushes his hat back and looks up at Jules. "When you hear 'bout a tough, pistol-packin' gringo youngster in these parts, chances are, yer behind it."

"It sure is a relief to see you, Hobbs."

Jules uncocks his pistol, gives it a twirl, and holsters it. Then, he dismounts and pulls the colonel from the saddle. Ranger Hobbs hooks a thumb in his belt and looks them over. "What have ya got there?"

Francisco offers, "This is the one they call *The Colonel*. The man who I told you has caused all these problems."

The colonel puffs out his chest and addresses everyone. "I stand with the *law* in these parts."

Shaking his head, Francisco retorts, "Only the law that you *purchase* with the railroad's *money*."

Jules looks at the two rangers by the barn door and then back to Hobbs. "Where's Bentley…?"

"He's in Austin right now tryin' to get us paid. I'm up here overseein' a Ranger Camp."

Francisco points eastward. "Debajo, Colorado." Jules is confused, until the rancher adds, "Their camp setup, near to the big river, is named for it coming from, and being below the place called Colorado."

Ranger Hobbs asks, "Jules, weren't you headed for Colorado the last time I saw ya?"

"We got sidetracked…"

Hobbs surveys the homestead and shrugs. "Gosh, if this is as far as ya made it, ya sure didn't get far." Barking from the other side of a hill grabs his attention, and Dog comes running from the direction of town. "Holy smokes…! Is that the dog?"

At full tilt, Dog races toward them. Hobbs notices a slight hitch in the canine's gait and remembers the incident with the arrow. Smiling at the sight of the dog, he asks, "Where's yer pal, Holton?" Then, not far behind, Holton comes galloping over the hill. "I'll be damned… Speak of the devil."

Holton charges at them and, upon reaching the barn, brings his horse to a skidding stop. In a cloud of dust, he leaps from the saddle with rifle in hand. He quickly recognizes Francisco and Ranger Hobbs. "Buenos Días, Señor Garcia. Good to see you here, Ranger!"

Looking to the other two Texas Rangers, and then back at Hobbs, Holton asks, "Is this all you have with you?"

The ranger studies Holton's sweat-streaked horse and looks back at the buckskin-clad westerner. "Was I s'posed to bring more?"

"Would come in handy."

Puzzled, they all stare at Holton for a moment, until the ground rumbles with the hoofbeats of approaching horses. They look to the hill Holton just came from and see riders charging toward the homestead. The colonel smiles gleefully, as Holton ushers them all into the barn. "We best git inside…"

Ranger Hobbs asks, "Who are those guys?"

Holton gestures to the colonel. "They come for *him*."

"Why?"

Del Rio Hondo

Coolly, Holton utters, "It's complicated…"

From the open doorway, Hobbs watches the mob of bounty hunters get closer. He looks over to see Jules draw his sidearm and move to one of the wood-shuttered windows. Aiming the barrel of his pistol outside, Jules calls out to him. "Ranger Hobbs, git inside!"

Counting the approaching horsemen, the ranger asks, "Why don't we just give 'im up?"

Seeing Sheriff Lowe and Rickter at the head of the mob, Jules responds, "Then they would kill us for sure."

"Really…?"

Smugly, the colonel looks to the approaching horde. "Either way, you'll all be dead soon enough."

Using the broadside of his rifle, Holton pushes the colonel deeper into the barn. "We all get dead someday."

Chapter 40

Everyone inside the barn finds a vantage point to defend. Positioned in the loft, Francisco peeks out the hay door. "If we need to leave pronto, the corral is clear."

Holton pokes his head out for a brief look around. "They're circling the place and will have us surrounded."

Opening the wood shutters slightly, Jules points his pistol through and peers outside. "Heck, if we leave here now, it will just be a running fight."

Standing near the door, Ranger Hobbs shakes his head. "I don't do *runnin'* fights, 'less *I'm* doin' the *chasin'*."

Holton pulls the door partly closed after Dog rushes in, and then he levers his rifle. "You can chase 'em if ya want."

Amused, Ranger Hobbs looks at Holton and levers a round into his own rifle. "What's with you and that durn kid? Yer both sure to find trouble, as sure as I find saloons."

As the riders slow their approach, Holton speaks aside to Hobbs. "Ain't lookin' for it... Suppose it just comes natural."

While Rickter and Sheriff Lowe bark out orders, the bounty hunters encircle the barn, dismount, and take up shooting positions. Hobbs asks Holton. "Who's that givin' orders out there?"

Holton studies the men outside. "That fella with the badge is a local sheriff, and the one to his left works for *him*." He nods toward the colonel.

"A lawman is out there?"

"Bought and paid for."

"Might be they'd negotiate with a Texas Ranger?"

"Doubt it..."

Ranger Hobbs does a count of the armed men outside. "We're outnumbered three to one."

"Seems that way."

"Them aren't good odds."

"For *us* or *them*...?"

Hobbs gives Holton a sarcastic look. "Us... Ya figure different?"

Del Rio Hondo

Keeping behind the heavy wooden door, Holton shrugs. "I like our odds in here much better than being out *there*."

Ranger Hobb scoots alongside Holton, looks outside, and hands him his rifle. "Here, hold this…"

With his pistol poking out the window, Jules watches Ranger Hobbs step out, leaving Holton at the doorway holding both rifles. "Where's he going?"

"To negotiate…"

The colonel grins. "Good luck…"

Jules gives the colonel a cold stare and then turns to watch Hobbs, hands raised, walk out from the barn.

All is quiet, as the posse pauses to watch the lone figure coming out of the barn. Taking note of their positions, the ranger clears his throat and addresses them. "Hello, fellas… What seems to be the problem here?"

The sheriff, gesturing for Rickter and the others to stand down, replies, "Who are you?"

"I'm a Texas Ranger."

"How many more are inside?"

"Enough."

After eyeing the few horses in the corral, the sheriff exchanges a look with Rickter and then calls out to Hobbs. "How 'bout you fellers do yer job… Release the colonel, then hand over Holton Lang and the boy."

Hobbs glances back at the barn. "What for?"

Rickter calls out, "So we can hang 'em."

Looking toward Rickter, Hobbs lowers his arms a bit. "We can take 'em to Fort Worth for a proper trial."

Sheriff Lowe responds, "What about the colonel?"

"Is that the fella with them?"

"That's right... Set him loose, and we'll consider lettin' you be on yer way."

Ranger Hobbs notices Rickter making eye contact with several men, directing them to position themselves for a fight. He feels a trickle of sweat form up and slide down his temple. "We better take him with us, so he can testify at their trial." Sensing them readying to strike, he takes a step backward.

One last time, Sheriff Lowe offers, "Release the colonel, or we end this all right here and now."

"I'm a *Texas Ranger*..."

"You mentioned that."

With multiple firearms pointed in his direction, Hobbs takes another step backward. Noticing Rickter's smirking grin, he takes a breath and continues to negotiate. "Call off yer men, or you'll be charged accordin'ly."

There is dead silence, until the sheriff finally responds. "Charged by *who*...?"

Rickter lifts his rifle to his shoulder, takes aim, and squeezes the trigger. At the same time, Hobbs jumps back, drawing his sidearm. The two shots are fired simultaneously, Rickter's hitting Hobbs along the vest, and Hobbs' nicking Rickter just above the top of his boot. The ranger dashes inside, and the fight commences. From all sides, gunshots smash into the barn, throwing puffs of dust and chunks of mud-brick.

Chapter 41

Jules ducks down as bullets crash through the windows. Holton grabs the injured ranger, pulls him inside and swings the door shut. "Where're you hit, Ranger?"

With adrenaline pumping through his system, Hobbs looks down at several bloody marks on his clothing. "Dagnabbit…! Where *ain't* I hit?!?"

Holton drags the ranger to the middle of the barn and props him up against a support beam. He assesses Hobbs' wounds, as hot rounds of lead continue to slam into the thick adobe walls and tear through the wooden doors and shutters. "You got lucky, Ranger… I don't think any bullets are in ya. Merely scratches…"

Ranger Hobbs winces. "*Lucky* ain't what comes t'mind."

Holton pats him on the arm and then offers Hobbs' rifle. "You'll be fine. Can you shoot?"

Taking his long gun from Holton, Hobbs grumbles, "Darnation… I'd rather be holdin' a bottle."

"Looks to be, you've had enough shots already."

The ranger rolls his eyes at the grim humor and lays his rifle across his lap. "How long can we hole-up here?"

Holton looks to Jules at the window and then to the two other rangers. "We're set up to hold them off a while."

"How 'bout food 'n water?"

Holton calls up to Francisco. "Señor Garcia…"

Reloading his shotgun, the Spaniard peers down from the loft. When Holton waves him closer, the rancher slides down a rope to join him. "Que pasa?"

"What kind of supplies do you have in here?"

Francisco smiles and heads to the back corner of a stall. Sweeping a pile of straw aside, he reveals a hidden door flush with the ground. He taps the toe of his boot on the wood panel. "This is our root cellar. We can stay inside this barn and be comfortably fed for a week."

Holton and Hobbs exchange a glance of satisfaction. Looking down at his handgun and rifle, the ranger inquires, "Any ammunition…?"

Francisco frowns and shakes his head. "Lo siento, no… Only loose powder and lead for a musket that is down there…"

Holton stands and looks back to Jules shooting outside. "With any luck, we won't need that." He moves to the window, as Jules aims and takes a shot. "How's it look out there, kid?"

Jules pulls back from the window, leans on the mud-brick wall, and empties the spent cartridges from his gun. "There's quite a few out there, and their plan seems to be to throw enough lead to knock this barn down."

Pressing his hand against the wall, Holton comments, "These adobe walls will hold up. Save your shots."

Jules finishes reloading, and then looks at Holton with complete sincerity. "I'm sorry for getting you into this mess."

Holton offers a consoling nod. "When ya do the right thing, there's no need fer apologies."

With the seasoned westerner's approval, Jules feels an uplifting sense of pride. He watches as Holton keeps low under the sporadic zing of bullets, working his way to the positions of the other Texas Rangers.

~*~

As the afternoon wears on, the shooting continues at a steady pace. Clouds of black-powder smoke fill the air, punctuated by the sharp reports of firearms, and the thuds of lead projectiles slapping into mud-brick walls. With their men occasionally jockeying for better position, the mob keeps the adobe barn surrounded.

Eventually evening sets in, and the interior of the barn is dimly lit by streaks of waning light. Long shadows conceal the once-obvious targets. An occasional bullet rips through the building but, for the most part, the shooting has tapered-off. Seeing Hobbs propped peacefully against the post, Jules thinks, for an instant, that the ranger has passed. But, then the ranger winces and repositions himself. Easing in alongside Jules, Holton sits himself against the wall. "How're ya doin', kid?"

"Fine… For now."

"You okay on cartridges?"

The youth nods and, through the dim light, looks at Holton. "What happens when it gets dark?"

"They'll either rush us or wait till morning."

"What do you think they'll do?"

Holton shrugs and slides more cartridges into the side loading gate of his rifle. "All depends on how many of 'em have families to go home to."

"Or, what the bounty on us is…"

Holton silently nods. Trying to lift the conversation, Jules notices Francisco feeding the wounded ranger some canned food from the cellar. "It's good to have Ranger Hobbs around again, eh?"

"Bet there are places he'd rather be…"

"Is he shot up bad?"

"He'll heal in time."

Jules takes a breath and rubs a finger alongside his nose. "If we have much left of it…"

As the darkness slowly spreads over the homestead, Holton props himself up to look out the window. He spots a few cookfires and notes a lantern light coming from the cabin. "They look to be settling in for the night. Keep listening for any movement from out there." Moving into a squatted position, Holton pats the boy's shoulder. "You stay here. I'll tell the ranger in the loft to take a free shot, if someone happens to pass in front of the firelight."

Jules grins. "I was thinking the same."

Standing, Holton takes one last peek out the window. "Hang tight, kid… We'll come out of this yet."

Holton scoots across the barn to talk with Hobbs and then moves over to the other rangers.

Chapter 42

Campfires cast an eerie, flickering light on the bullet-riddled barn as men outside cook meager rations over sheltered flames. Occasional shadows cross the lit windows of the cabin, as those inside gather round the table to discuss their options.

Sheriff Lowe sits across from Rickter. Behind them, another man, holding a rifle in the crook of his arm, paces the hard-packed dirt floor. Lowe shakes his head at Rickter. "Murder *ain't* what I signed-up for."

In the dimness, Rickter glares at the reluctant lawman. "Sheriff, ya signed up for whatever we pay ya for."

"My orders come from the colonel, not you."

Del Rio Hondo

"Then, gettin' him back safe should be a concern of yers."

The sheriff snaps at the deputy that's pacing the room. "Sit *down,* will ya? Yer makin' me nervous."

The man stops his uneasy march and stares at the sheriff, while Rickter continues. "There's only a few of 'em in there. Figger, we could rush 'em now. In the cover of darkness... We'd be done with it all by mornin'."

"I thought you wanted the colonel outta here alive?"

Rickter pauses, and then with a wicked smile, he adds, "It's a chance I'd be willin' to take."

"That's 'cause yer not the one bein' held *captive* in there." Unconcerned, Rickter shrugs and glances to the door, while the sheriff continues. "I say we wait till dawn 'nd close in on them at first light. They'll be tired, and we'll have the advantage."

Rickter rests his palms on the worn surface of the table. "Could still get 'im killed... *Accidental,* like."

Unyielding, Sheriff Lowe continues. "Rickter, it's yer job to make sure that doesn't happen."

A gun fires outside, and a window curtain flutters. Displaying a pained expression, the deputy with the rifle looks down at the bloody, bullet wound to his abdomen He crumples to the floor, as Rickter and Lowe glare at each other until the sheriff leans over to snuff out the lantern.

~*~

Light streams in through the array of holes in the barn door as the sky brightens with a new day. His hands in his lap, the colonel sits across from the watchful stare of Hobbs. Uncomfortable, the colonel looks away and then back again. "What are you staring at?"

"Jest tryin' to figure out what sort of man would be the cause of all of this trouble."

"If folks simply did what they were told, there wouldn't be any trouble to be had."

Hobbs nods drunkenly and lifts a brown-tinted bottle, near-empty, from his lap. After a long swig, he belches under his breath. "It's city-folks like you who really chap my hide. Tellin' everyone what to do and how to live."

The colonel watches him swish what remains in the bottle, while taking note of the ranger's numerous wounds. "You're in need of medical attention. And drunk..."

"Jest drunk 'nough to see the truth..."

Holton and Jules come from the other side of the barn to squat down next to Hobbs. Holton checks the inadequate bandaging, grimly realizing that it will have to do for now. "How're ya doin', Ranger?"

Ranger Hobbs takes another drink. "Fine, I s'pose."

Holton looks at Jules. "What are you smilin' at, kid?"

"I was expectin' some of that whiskey to spring out from all them holes he has in 'im."

Holton frowns. "Who gave him the bottle?"

"Señor Garcia found it in the cellar."

Holton looks up to the ranger in the hay loft and then to the other one guarding the entryway. Across the barn, Francisco stares out a window, resting his shotgun on the ledge. "If they're comin', it'll be soon. Jules, you stay here and watch these two."

Hobbs drunkenly protests. "I don't need a *baby-sitter*."

Tilting his head toward the colonel, Holton states, "Maybe not, but *he* does."

The colonel glares at Holton. "You'll hang yet, Lang."

Taking a seat on an empty wooden crate next to Hobbs, Jules directs his pistol at the prisoner. "You won't live to see it."

Looking around at the bullet-riddled doors and window shutters, the colonel shakes his head. "You can't *possibly* think you'll get out of here *alive...*"

Jules gives his pistol a twirl on his finger and then points it back at the colonel. "How nice of you to care about us... S'pecially, when you should be worried 'bout yer own hide."

Keeping down low, Holton moves to the front doorway. Colonel Henry purses his lips and silently watches.

Chapter 43

The sheriff's men creep into attack positions, taking any available cover to be found. As the sun peeks over the horizon, the men aim their guns in preparation for their final assault. Suddenly, a loud bellow erupts from the western hills, accompanied by the distinct sound of galloping horses.

Pausing their planned attack, they turn to see a lone supply wagon charging down the hill. Bear slaps the harness reins and lets out another whooping holler. "*Hiyaaaaaaa!!!*" Bear glances back into the box of the wagon and calls out, "Keep down there, missy…"

Alice, nestled amongst the supplies and holding a rifle at the ready, looks outside through a rolled-up canvas flap. "You keep drivin' this wagon, and I'll take care of myself."

Next to her, aiming his sawed-off shotgun out the other side, Ernesto grips a rib of the canopy frame for support. "Vámonos! We are ready. You say when, Señor Bear."

"Stay ready... We're almost on 'em..."

The wagon races down the hill, and several bounty hunters pop out of concealment and stare at the new arrivals. A shot rings out, and then gunfire explodes from both sides. The wagon rushes toward the barn and swings around. Whooping and howling, Bear steers the wagon in a wide circle around the barn, flushing men from hiding. A mix of dust and black powder smoke fills the air, masking the early morning sunshine with a cloudy, orange haze.

On Bear's third pass around the yard, the bullet-riddled door of the barn swings open, and Holton steps outside. Hastily, he takes a shot, levers his rifle and yells. "Bear, get that wagon inside here, 'fore you bust yer stitches!!!"

Steering the lathered team toward the door, Bear reaches his foot up to the brake lever. He stands on it, as he pulls back on the reins. The wagon skids along behind the running animals, through the wide entryway and on into the barn. Holding the team back, he brings the wagon to a jarring halt. As the dust settles, Bear scans the dimly lit interior. Grinning from ear to ear, he asks, "Where the heck are the rest of ya?"

Holton steps up alongside the wagon. "Rest of *who...*?"

Del Rio Hondo

Rubbing a tickle of dirt from his whiskers, Bear grunts, "We was stopped o'er yonder that hill yesterday afternoon, and it sounded like a second Antietam."

In good humor, Hobbs raises his bottle and chuckles. "Just us merry gents…"

After throwing a wink at Holton, Bear climbs down from the wagon and goes over to the Texas Ranger to accept the offered bottle. Tipping it back. he takes the last swallow. "Thanks. Ya got any more of this?"

Holton shoots Francisco a scolding glance. *"No…"* Turning back to Bear, he asks, "What're you doing here?"

As Bear tips the bottle way back to finish the last drop, a bullet smashes through it, leaving only the neck in his hand. Tossing it aside, he looks at Holton. "We come to rescue you, pardner…" He scrunches his beard in a comical way. "Again."

Ernesto hops from the back of the wagon, breaks open his shotgun and reloads it. Holton stares at him for a moment and then looks back to Bear. "You left her *alone?*"

Bear innocently crinkles his brow, as he watches Jules help the pregnant woman down from the rear of the wagon. Holton turns to see her and gasps, "You brought her *here?*"

Bear sputters, "How would I know ya'd have a whole damn army after ya? Besides, she's not a woman you can jest tell what to do and stay put."

Holding her midsection, Alice stands before Holton. "Bear didn't have a choice in the matter. I was coming whether he came along or not." Holton turns to Bear who displays a look of virtue.

While the gunfire outside continues, Holton, frustrated, heaves a breath and walks away. Bear shrugs, looks around and then smiles at Alice. "How's that for a howdy-do welcome..." As Alice and Ernesto take up shooting positions at an available window, Bear looks down at the Texas Ranger. "Hey pardner, got any more of that who-hit-John?"

Ranger Hobbs smiles drunkenly and gives a broad wink. "Nope... But, I know where we can find more of it."

Jules smiles at the pair of carousers while keeping his gun aimed at the colonel. "Good to see you again, Bear."

Bear's friendly grin beams through his bushy beard. "Good to see ya again too, kid."

~*~

The siege comes to a standstill with only occasional shots being fired from either side. At the doorway of the cabin, Rickter and Sheriff Lowe duck out of the home. Keeping low, they peer over a low adobe wall and analyze the sturdy barn. The sheriff is the first to speak up. "They ain't gonna come out, and we don't have enough food to feed these men."

"I wasn't plannin' on a picnic..."

The sheriff glares sideways at Rickter. "Come noontime, I'm leavin' with what men I got left. They'll release the colonel eventually if we let them be."

Del Rio Hondo

Rickter thinks on it a moment and then shakes his head. "I'm not leavin' this place without the satisfaction of havin' my way with them inside."

"What about those that jest come in the wagon?"

"They're signed up fer the same, in *my* book."

A bullet pings off the top of the mud brick wall, sending a spray of dirt over the two men. Lowe removes his hat and dusts it off. "This is *ridiculous…*"

"Gimme another hour… I'll organize a plan to rush 'em and end all this fer good."

The sheriff takes out his pocket watch, flips open the cover and looks at the time. "Okay… *One hour…*"

Chapter 44

Sporadic gunfire echoes across the ranch yard. Inside the barn, as Alice dresses a fresh bullet wound on one of the Texas Rangers, she aims a scolding glare toward Hobbs and Bear. "Now, Bear... Who gave you *that?*"

Bear smiles, passing the whiskey bottle to Hobbs. "Medicinal purposes only, ma'am..."

"For *who...?*" Bear grins even wider and points a finger at the drunk ranger.

Alice shakes her head in admonishment, finishes the bandaging and attempts to stand. Suddenly, she winces in pain and drops to her knees. Bear jumps up and rushes to her side. "You okay, missy...?"

"No... This baby wants to come out."

Del Rio Hondo

Unsure of what to do, Bear looks to Ranger Hobbs and the bottle. "How 'bout a shot of rye to *relax* the kid?"

As Bear helps her to stand, Alice shakes her head. "*No…!* And, no more for *you*, either."

"What…? *Why?!?*"

Alice looks to where Holton is tucked-in by the front door with his rifle aimed outside. Then, deadly serious, she turns to Bear. "You're gonna help me have this *baby*."

"*WHAT?!?*"

He unwillingly follows her, as she tugs him toward a pile of straw in the back corner of the barn. "You've helped around the ranch…"

"Yeah, with *cattle* and a few *horses*… There's no way…! Ya *cain't* have the baby in *here*."

"Why not…? *Jesus* did it."

"Heck, he done *a lotta stuff* that I wouldn't do."

"Quit your whining and get some water."

After looking around in an unsuccessful bid for help, Bear helps Alice lay down on the makeshift bedding.

~*~

Under intermittent gunfire, Rickter makes the rounds, ordering his men to get ready for another assault on the barn. As he scurries back to where the sheriff hides behind the block wall, he hears a muffled scream coming from the barn. Ducking down, he is met with a confused look from the sheriff. "Was that a *woman's* scream?"

Rickter peeks over the wall and toward the barn. "Yeah... So what?"

"How did a damn *woman* get in there?"

"Who cares...?"

"I didn't sign up for this."

When the sheriff gets up to leave, Rickter jabs the barrel of his pistol into his stomach. "Set yerself back down, Sheriff. You ain't goin' nowhere..."

In disbelief, Sheriff Lowe glances down at the gun, and Rickter pulls back the hammer. Then he clenches his jaw and growls at Rickter. "I through... I *ain't* gonna murder a *woman!* Or, have *any* part in harmin' *children.*"

Rickter forces a grin. "Too bad ya got morals all 'a sudden... Yer part of this. And, yer here till it's finished."

Sheriff Lowe pushes the gun away. "No..." He starts to stand up again. "Not anymore..." The blast of the pistol is lost in the surrounding gunfire. Lowe crumples, as smoke billows from the barrel. Incredulous, he stares at Rickter, as he slumps to the side.

"Sorry, but ya asked fer it, pal..." Giving a whistle, Rickter stands and waves his smoking pistol toward the barn. In unison, the attackers leap from hiding, firing their weapons as they charge the barn.

Just inside the barn door, Holton is loading more cartridges into his rifle. When he hears the whistle, he looks up. "Here they come!" Putting his rifle to his shoulder, he aims, snaps off a shot, levers the gun, and shoots again.

Del Rio Hondo

Jules sees the others rush to the doors and windows, determined to defend their holdout as best they can. Addressing the colonel, he cocks back the hammer of his pistol. "As soon as one of your men comes into this barn, yer dead."

The colonel nervously stares at the young man, as the sunlight gradually fills with hazy gun smoke.

~*~

As the onslaught continues, several men fall wounded before reaching the barn. Some make it to the brick walls and use them for cover from the guns inside. They creep to the doors and windows of the barn, preparing to break in.

Holton fires again. He levers another round into the chamber and looks back to Bear. "How's she doin'?"

Bear wipes sweat from Alice's brow, as she tries to muffle her screams. "Not great... *She's havin' a baby!!!*"

"Tell her to hold on..."

While Alice groans and puffs for breath, Bear yells, "Dammit, Holton...! It's *yer* kid! *You* tell 'er!"

Two men push through the door. Holton quickly shoots one and then grapples with the other. When yet another one comes in, Jules instinctively points his revolver and fires. As the man tumbles aside, Jules turns back to see that the colonel is off and running for the door to the corral.

Jules quickly fires and misses, just as the colonel rushes past a wounded Texas Ranger. Jules yells to him, "*Stop* 'im...! He's gonna get *away*..." Jules looks back as Holton is still grappling with the second intruder. Then, he gets to his feet and races after the colonel.

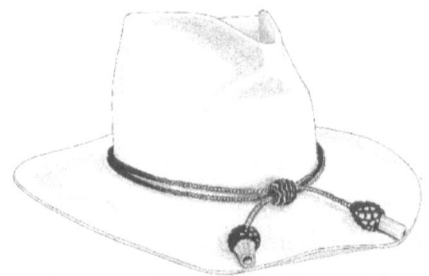

Chapter 45

Rushing past the bounty hunters about to enter the barn through the side door, the colonel screams, "Kill them all...!!! He dashes to one of the saddled horses at the far end of the corral and leaps aboard. Kicking his heels, he looks back, just as Jules comes out of the barn to face the three men.

In quick succession, Jules puts a bullet in each of them and only receives a grazing wound in return. He turns to see the colonel flee through the corral gate and bolt toward town. Holstering his pistol, Jules runs to Francisco's mount and leaps aboard. He jabs his spurred heels and is quickly in pursuit.

As they race from the ranch toward town, a new group of riders comes from the other direction, firing their guns and yipping like wild Indians. Holton steps out of the barn, turns, and shoots from the hip, hitting a man charging at him.

Then, he notices the youth galloping after the colonel. He looks again to the approaching riders and tries to discern whether they are hostile or friendly. But, his attention is drawn to movement in the corral, where someone else is mounting up. Following after Jules and the colonel, the rider spins his horse and heads for the open gate. "*Rickter…*"

~*~

Using the quickest route back to the town, the colonel rides along the steep banks of the river. Jules is nearly matching the speed of the fleeing rider, but he is unable to overtake him. As Jules rides full tilt, he looks down at the riata attached to the side of the saddle and unfastens Francisco's coil of rope. Jules makes a loop and twirls it over his head. Chasing the colonel, he spurs his horse to get closer.

Finally, he throws the rope, and the wide loop sails through the air but misses. Jules curses under his breath, rides past the limp line and recoils the riata. The colonel's horse momentarily falters from its pace, and Jules begins to close the distance. With fear in his eyes, the colonel looks back at the pursuing rider and slaps the horse's rump.

Jules swings another loop over his head a few times, takes aim, and tosses it forward. This time, it lands over the head and shoulders of its intended target. Frantically, the colonel tries to push the riata off, but Jules pulls his mount back and skids to a stop.

As the rope tightens around his neck and arm, the colonel jerks on his horse's bit causing his animal to rear up, twist, and tumble down the embankment. In a flurry of motion and screams, the horse and rider disappear from sight and the riata is yanked from Jules' grasp.

Steering his mount over to the edge of the riverbank, Jules looks down to see the uninjured saddle horse struggle to its feet and shake off the fall. Closer in to the embankment, the riata is tangled in the protruding roots and branches of a tree. The colonel dangles with a twisted arm and neck, his polished city-boots nearly touching the sandy shore. With a few slight jerks of movement, his life departs.

Deeply satisfied with the colonel's death, Jules stares for a while before looking away. As he turns his mount to leave, Jules comes face to face with Rickter. Moving his horse closer to the embankment, the mercenary peers over the steep cliff. "Ya think he's dead?"

Startled, Jules quickly shakes it off and coolly responds, "He got what he deserved."

"*Yer* about to git *yers...!*" Rickter swings his fist out and punches Jules in the face. Before Jules can recover. Rickter hits him again and continues to smash his fist into the young man.

Jules tumbles to the ground and spits blood. Winded, and his vision blurred, he looks past his horse up to Rickter. "I'll *kill* you..."

Del Rio Hondo

Resting his hand on the butt of his pistol, Rickter grins. "I've heard that before... I think it's all jest the idle talk of a blow-hard kid."

Sitting up, Jules glances down and realizes that his gun is still in its holster. His horse moves aside, and when Jules looks up at Rickter again, the man laughs. "Go ahead, kid... Jerk that shooter. I'd like to see you make an effort to kill me." Rickter chuckles again and draws his pistol. He slowly cocks the hammer, waves it at Jules, and snorts, "What's the matter? Ya lost yer nerve, kid?"

Recounting the shots he fired previously, Jules considers his grim options. Then, quick as lightning, he draws his pistol and cocks back the hammer. Just as he pulls the trigger, another gunshot fires. Rickter remains frozen in the saddle, his pistol yet to be fired. He looks down to where two bullets have passed through him, one from the front and one from the back.

Dropping his gun, Rickter slowly slumps down from his mount into a heap on the ground. As Jules cocks his pistol again, he sees Holton coming up from behind. The buckskin-clad westerner twirl-cocks his rifle and steps from his horse. "Figured you had him alright kid... But wanted to be sure."

Worse for wear, Jules climbs to his feet and smears away the blood on his face. Holton inspects Rickter's dead body and then walks toward Jules. The youngster rushes to Holton and hugs him tightly. "I'm *always* glad to see you, Holton."

Holding the boy close, Holton looks to the tangle of rope bunched up in the brush and trailing over the embankment. "Glad to see you too, kid."

After a lengthy embrace, Jules pulls back and remarks, "The colonel is dead."

Holton glances to where Rickter lies slumped at the feet of the horse. "Him, too…"

"What about the others?"

"We should be gettin' back."

Chapter 46

The battle on the Garcia homestead has ended, and several men guard the sheriff's posse. As Holton and Jules arrive, they are greeted by the Texas Ranger, Captain Bentley. Curiously studying them as they approach, the ranger decides to address the younger man first. "Hello, Mister Ward..." Jules flashes a grin when he recognizes the ranger. "And, Holton Lang... Figured the both of you couldn't stay out of trouble for long..."

Holton, still holding his rifle, rides up next to Bentley and steps off his horse. "We were sure glad to see you fellas show up when you did."

Jules asks, "How'd you know where to find us?"

Eric H. Heisner

"Upon my return to the Ranger camp from Austin, there was a very determined woman with her young daughter who had an odd story to tell."

"Yeah...?"

"Said they had orders from Hobbs to come here with a passel of Texas Rangers, if he wasn't back in two days."

"They led you here?"

"Eager to get back, and were difficult to keep up with."

Holton looks at the bullet-scarred barn. "How's Hobbs?"

The ranger gives Holton a wry look. "Drunk..."

"Better'n dead..."

"He's too ornery to get dead."

With his sleeves rolled up, Bear steps out from the barn, and Holton greets him with a nod. "I know a fella like that..." When the old friends make eye contact, Bear shakes his head. Assuming the worst, Holton makes way for the barn. Reaching Bear, he lowers his voice. "What's happened? How is she?"

Bear's head shaking stops, and a smile breaks through his grizzled features. "The things ya do in a barn..."

Behind him, Francisco's wife comes out holding a newborn wrapped in a cloth sack. "Are you the father?"

Putting his hands up, Bear steps aside. "Not *me!*"

Speechless, Holton nods, and she hands him the baby. He looks down at the swaddled infant and then back to the Mexican woman. "What *is* it?"

Bear guffaws. "That's a *baby*, dummy."

228

Del Rio Hondo

Holton shoots a quick glare at Bear and then looks back to Leticia. She responds, "You have a healthy son."

He smiles down at the child and then peers into the barn. "How is his mother…?"

"She is resting."

Light streaming in through numerous bullet holes dimly illuminates the barn, as Holton enters. He goes to the corner where Alice, lying on the straw bed, is being cared for by Alejandra. With apprehension, the young girl looks up and asks, "Is Jules okay?"

She is relieved when Holton tilts his head toward the group of men outside. "He's fine… He could maybe use your special attentions for a busted lip." Bursting with joy, Alejandra springs to her feet and rushes outside. With the baby in his arms, Holton looks down at the mother. Then, he takes a knee. "Ya got a good-lookin' son here…"

Pale and sweaty, Alice smiles at Holton. She wipes wet hair from her forehead and stares up at him with bright eyes. "Strong and determined. Like his pa." When Bear coughs, standing in the doorway, Holton turns to look at him. Alice swats his arm to turn him back to her. "Not *him*, you dolt…!" He nods thoughtfully and gently places the baby in her arms.

Jules, Alejandra, Ernesto, Captain Bentley, and Ranger Hobbs all gather at the doorway to watch. Holton touches a finger alongside the tiny baby's cheek. "Does he have a name?"

She fondly looks down at the infant. "If you don't have an objection, I'd like to call him *William Holton Lang.*"

Holton bows his head. "That's a *fine* name for the boy." He smiles. "Maybe we'll call him *Bear-cub* for short."

Unamused, Alice sternly shakes her head at Holton. "You most *certainly* will *not.*"

He shrugs. "Then, how 'bout *Willie?*"

"We'll talk about it…"

Happy to have Alejandra dotting over him, Jules looks at Bear and chuckles. Then, looking outside, past the rangers, to see Francisco and Leticia reuniting at the cabin, he feels a rush of familial contentment. He enters the barn, approaches Holton and places his hand on the kneeling man's shoulder. "William is a good name with a lot of potential."

"*I'll drink to that…!*" Leaning against the door frame, barely able to stand, Hobbs jangles his spurs, lifts a fresh bottle, takes a swig, and passes it over to Ernesto. "*Cheers…!*"

Bear gets the bottle from them next and takes a swallow. "And, so will I…"

The End…

If you enjoyed **Del Río Hondo**,
read other stories by

Eric H. Heisner

www.leandogproductions.com

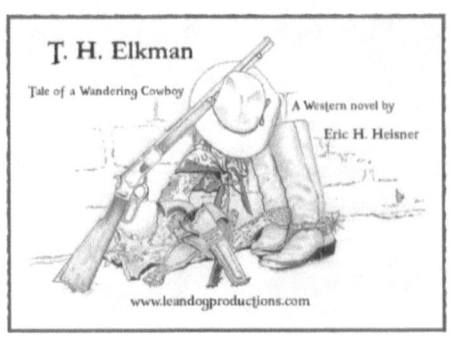

Eric H. Heisner is an award-winning writer, actor, and filmmaker. He is the author of several Western and Adventure novels: *West to Bravo, T. H. Elkman, Africa Tusk, Conch Republic,* and *Short Western Tales: Friend of the Devil.*
He can be contacted at his website:
www.leandogproductions.com

Al P. Bringas is a cowboy artist, actor, and horse lover. He had done illustrations for novels including, *T. H. Elkman,* the *West to Bravo* series, *Wings of the Pirate* and *Mexico Sky.* He lives and works in Pasadena, California.